Belle Man up on the wrong side of the bed. **But she wasn't used to waking up in the wrong bed entirely.**

It was the type of room that Belle would expect someone like Darryl Horak to sleep in. That was the worst insult she could think of.

Heavens, her head hurt. It wasn't like her to drink too much. And who owned that massive, bare, totally hunky body lying in bed next to her? Belle had been trying to ignore the lug, but he didn't seem likely to go away. She had a great view of his broad shoulders and straight back.

She wished she remembered last night. They must have done *something* in here. She hoped she'd enjoyed it.

Maybe just the teensiest bit of a replay wouldn't go amiss. Anonymous couplings weren't Belle's style, but there was no hurry to shut the barn door once the horse had escaped.

A smile creeping across her face, Belle leaned over him and blew gently onto his stomach. The man's response was instantaneous, as he pulled her on top of him.

At that moment Belle got an unobstructed view of his face.

Darryl Horak!

Dear Reader,

A new year always brings lots of new friends and new opportunities into our lives. At LOVE & LAUGHTER we are especially proud of the number of new writers we have discovered. One of the greatest joys an editor can have is making "the call"—telling a hopeful, unpublished author, "We love your book and want to buy it."

Tracy South is one of those new voices. She is also the winner of the LOVE & LAUGHTER contest. Her book is a real delight, both witty and romantic. Other new voices in the months ahead include Stephanie Bond, Bonnie Tucker, Trish Jensen and Colleen Collins. I'm sure you'll enjoy their stories as much as we did and look for books by these fresh, new funny ladies.

Prolific and always popular Jacqueline Diamond delivers a knockout punch in the hilarious *Punchline*. This story about rival editors from competing magazines, who just *despise* each other yet keep ending up together, is terrific. A classic battle of the sexes, set in the 1990s.

I hope the New Year brings you much love and laughter.

Malle Vallik

Malle Vallik
Associate Senior Editor

PUNCHLINE
Jacqueline Diamond

Harlequin Books

TORONTO • NEW YORK • LONDON
AMSTERDAM • PARIS • SYDNEY • HAMBURG
STOCKHOLM • ATHENS • TOKYO • MILAN
MADRID • WARSAW • BUDAPEST • AUCKLAND

ISBN 0-373-44011-1

PUNCHLINE

Copyright © 1997 by Jackie Hyman

Like my heroine's baby, my older son chose his own time to be born—in this case, ten weeks early. The mood in the delivery room was tense during the emergency Caesarean section. Out came my "huge" (4 lbs., 14 oz.) son, wailing at the top of his lungs. "There's nothing wrong with his lungs," cheered one nurse as she took him. "There's nothing wrong with his bladder," noted a second nurse, trying to diaper him. Then a third voice chimed in. "There's nothing wrong with his aim, either."

—Jacqueline Diamond

Special thanks to
Marcia Holman and Allison Joyce
for their help

1

BELLE MARTENS WAS used to waking up on the wrong side of the bed. But she wasn't used to waking up in the wrong bed entirely, in a room she had never seen before.

Her eyes snapped open and, before she knew it, she was critiquing the decor. Making clever disparaging remarks about her surroundings had become second nature to the editor of *Just Us* magazine.

And there was plenty to belittle in this room. What kind of macho idiot went in for wood paneling these days?

Not to mention the beige curtains covered with images of black-and-green mallards. The owner of this room must fancy himself a woodsman, when the closest he'd probably ever come to a duck was eating the Peking version in Chinatown.

It was the type of room that Belle would expect Darryl Horak to sleep in. That was the worst insult she could think of.

The readers of *Just Us,* a magazine for the woman of the nineties, were defined on the masthead as "sexy, secure and definitively single." They loathed the self-absorbed arrogant male represented by Darryl Horak and his egocentric magazine, *About Town.*

It was billed as being "For the man who has everything, and flaunts it." The owner of this room appeared to be a subscriber, as the magazine's monthly Flaunt It Girl centerfold hung on the wall. August was represented by an airbrushed brunette bursting the seams of her scarlet lingerie.

From outside came the murmur of surf and the scent of briny air. The owner of this house must be a beach bum. Belle felt **grateful** that, at least, her readers would never know she'd spent a night in such surroundings.

Heavens, her head hurt. She never drank to excess, so what could have happened? And who owned that massive, bare, totally hunky body lying in bed next to her?

Belle had been trying to ignore the lug, but he didn't seem likely to go away. She had a great view of his broad shoulders and straight back, and a wealth of sleep-mussed dark hair.

The whole package looked vaguely familiar, but she couldn't place him. This morning she wasn't sure she could place herself.

Maybe she could sneak out and not be noticed. There was a good chance that Mr. Hunk didn't remember any more about last night than she did.

Yet Belle knew that, as a sophisticated lady of the turn of the century, she needed to get the guy's vital statistics. Heck, she never did things like this, never, never.

She wished she remembered last night. They must have done *something* in here. She hoped she'd enjoyed it.

Maybe just the teensiest bit of a replay wouldn't go amiss. Anonymous couplings weren't Belle's style, but there was no hurry to shut the barn door once the horse had escaped.

She ran her fingers lightly along the man's back. He shifted and sighed.

The guy must spend hours at a gym. His muscles stood out, clearly defined, and his torso tapered to lean hips.

A glimmer of memory seeped into Belle's consciousness. Last night she'd attended a publicity party for a new rock group called Bend Your Mind—loud music, high-cholesterol food, some kind of fizzy, fruity punch.

The ambience had been pseudo high-tech. She recalled skinny female models wandering around wrapped in red plastic, and their bulked-up male counterparts posing with silver Mylar shirts unbuttoned down to the forbidden zone.

She must have landed one of those models, the masculine version. Very masculine. Belle wondered if Mr. Broad Shoulders had singled her out in hopes of getting featured in her magazine. But why had *she* gone home with *him*?

She remembered none of it. But why shouldn't she enjoy herself, now that she was here?

Aroused by her featherlike strokes, the man uttered a low moan and tossed from his side to his back, one arm draped across his face to block the daylight.

Belle knew she ought to get up. Just march into the bathroom, throw a little water on her face and skedaddle. This whole situation could prove messy and embarrassing, and while her public image bordered on flamboyance, she liked to call the shots.

On the other hand, the two of them were lying here stark naked. Belle had kept her distance from men since her engagement had exploded more than a year ago. It annoyed her to think she'd broken her fast with a stud like this and couldn't remember it.

Lying on his back, the guy provided a clear view of nature's bountiful offerings. Dark fur matted his chest. His stomach was flat and lean, his legs long and sturdy. She guessed he stood more than six feet tall, a good seven inches above her own height. But in bed, who cared?

She wished her blood weren't beginning to speed through her veins at the sight of him. She hated to think that she was attracted to the kind of guy who liked pictures of idealized, lingerie-clad women.

Not that there was anything wrong with Belle's figure, but she knew a photographer would consider her too short and round. And more than one critic had made snide remarks when, after her engagement bit the dust, Belle had dyed her brown hair a brassy red. She had meant it as a warning: Watch out for my temper.

She would never be deceived by a man again. So a brainless male model might be just what she needed to get back into the swing of dating. Horizontal dating, anyway.

A smile creeping across her face, Belle leaned over him and blew gently onto his stomach.

The man's response was instantaneous and unpredictable. One arm caught her waist and pulled her on top of him. The other seized her shoulder while his mouth clamped onto her breast, and his tongue stirred her nipple erect.

At that moment Belle got an unobstructed view of his face and nearly died of shock.

This was no pliant male model. This was Darryl Horak himself.

Darryl Horak: the self-styled man's man of the nineties, loud and relentless in his claim that women secretly wanted to be swept off their feet. The man was reputed to have dated every Flaunt It Girl featured in his magazine. He had also publicly termed Belle a frustrated lioness in need of taming.

This was the man whose mouth had claimed her other breast, and whose lips were now dashing from peak to peak, while his knee thrust between her legs and his arousal dug into her inner thigh.

She tried to protest, but Darryl had awakened in full heat. Effortlessly, he flipped her onto her back and his mouth closed over hers. Lower down, his hands spread her wide, ready to receive him.

Bucking hard against him, Belle realized her efforts were being taken for encouragement. There was no choice, none at all.

With an inward wince, she nipped his lower lip. When that failed to stop his determined thrusting toward the most vulnerable portion of her anatomy, she bit hard enough to draw blood.

A string of curses tore through the air. The man jerked away, hand pressed to his mouth in disbelief. "What the—?"

There was a sudden silence as their gazes entwined. Horror and shock registered on his high-boned face.

"Time to stop flaunting it—" Belle said, "—and put your pants on."

FOR A SERIES of first-person adventure articles, Darryl had raced a dogsled, dived among great white sharks and helped track a killer grizzly.

But in his wildest fantasy, he'd never pictured himself waking up next to a pit viper.

All right, maybe that was an excessive way to describe Belle Martens. She'd never actually poisoned anyone as far as he knew, but she had slashed more than a few people with her sharp tongue. And she'd just bitten him.

What the hell was she doing in his bed?

"First of all," he said, "I don't need to put on my pants because I live here."

"I'm glad you admit it," snapped the most exasperating woman in Los Angeles. "Because I intend to hold you fully responsible for kidnapping me and using me for your pleasure—completely against my will, I might add."

"What?" Darryl glared at her. He had never forced himself on a woman. "You flatter yourself."

"Deny it!" she challenged. How could the woman sit there in his bed, her breasts bare and her hair rioting around her face like a brushfire, without an ounce of self-consciousness?

Maybe it was an act. Darryl had sometimes wondered if Belle didn't exaggerate her toughness, just for effect.

"Deny what?"

"That you were panting all over me!"

He pressed one hand against his temple, which throbbed mercilessly. "I wake up passionate. Can I help it?"

"Are you trying to say you'd treat a pillow the same way?" she demanded.

His lips began to curl in an involuntary sneer, but were stopped by a tweak of pain where she'd bitten him. "Quit speaking as if you were addressing a jury, Belle. There's nobody here but us."

"And how exactly did that happen?" she snapped, loud enough to make his ears ache in counterpoint with his head.

"I don't have a clue." Not sure how to proceed, Darryl got up and went to the bathroom.

By the time he'd finished putting Neosporin on his lip, he had identified his final memory of the previous night: pouring himself some nonalcoholic punch at the press party and wondering why the stuff tasted so strange.

"We must have been done in by spiked punch," he said as he returned.

Belle was sitting on his bed, the covers draped around her waist. In these masculine quarters, she appeared smaller and more vulnerable than when he'd run into her at various press functions. Even that ridiculous dyed hair looked a bit more humorous than harsh in the morning light.

He'd better watch himself, Darryl reflected. If he wasn't careful, he might mistake Belle Martens for a human.

"If that's true, why wasn't anyone else affected?" she said.

"How do you know they weren't?" His gaze fell on the photo featuring Miss August and he wondered, involuntarily, how Belle would look in that particular piece of scarlet lingerie.

He couldn't imagine why he should care, not with all the women he had to choose from. Miss August had practically flung herself at Darryl after the photo session, but half an hour in her presence bored him half to death.

No one had ever called Belle Martens boring. That was one of the few pejoratives even Darryl wouldn't aim her way.

"So you think the guests are lying around all over Los Angeles, in bed with people they detest?" she said.

"Maybe they don't detest each other anymore," he suggested.

"You certainly didn't detest *me* this morning."

"Not until you bit me," he pointed out.

Belle flung back the covers and got out of bed. In all the years he and Belle had been trading insults, Darryl had never pictured how she would look naked. The scary part was that he liked it.

The breasts might be a bit oversize for her small frame. That was why, fully dressed, he'd considered her chunky. But her waist nipped inward in tantalizing fashion, and she had deliciously rounded buttocks. He could remember how she'd felt beneath him, soft and hot . . .

That was, of course, before she'd sunk her fangs into him. "Let's make a deal," he said.

Her eyebrow arched at him mistrustfully.

"We don't mention this to anyone," he proposed. "Assuming, of course, that there's anything to mention."

As he spoke, he remembered vaguely having a dream about Belle. A dream full of laughter, and tantalizing bosoms, and lots of sweaty wriggling between the sheets.

Oh, Lord. They'd definitely done it.

"There is nothing to mention." She marched past him, snatching pieces of clothing off a chair on her way to the bathroom. "Make some coffee, will you? I can't function until I have a cup. Sugar and milk, and none of that fake white powder, either.'' Her voice trailed behind, lingering after her corporeal self had disappeared.

Darryl grimaced. The possibility of revenge entered his mind: an article about a new wildlife adventure, this one pitting him against none other than Belle Martens.

Oh, hell. He didn't like to think about the descriptive passages with which she would skewer him in response. Besides, he prided himself on being something of a gentleman.

A truce, he thought. And, with any luck, a case of mutual amnesia.

Recognizing that sometimes it was best to yield to the inevitable, Darryl went to fix a pot of coffee.

THE GARGOYLE-OVERLAID clock on Belle's desk ticked relentlessly toward 11:00 a.m. It served to remind her that she'd accomplished precious little today.

Heck, she'd been working at a snail's pace since her encounter with Darryl Horak last month. She wished the man wouldn't keep intruding into her thoughts, with his big strong body and tight butt, and that wry way of regarding her that smacked of both arrogance and appreciation.

She grimaced and thrust him from her mind.

Articles and computer diskettes lay stacked on her broad desk, along with packets from models' agents urging her to feature their clients in photo shoots. The almost-final copy of the November issue needed board corrections before the computer files could be transferred onto a huge disk to ship to the printer. And Belle didn't feel like doing any of it.

She eyed a cake doughnut on her desk. Why was she so ravenous in the middle of the morning? The past few days, her stomach had felt like a black hole that might suck her inside if she didn't keep stuffing herself.

She took a bite and forced herself to chew slowly, hoping she would expend enough calories in the effort to forestall a weight gain. Even in September, Southern California weather remained summerlike, and she needed to keep in shape for a swimsuit.

Maybe it was the temptingly warm light filtering through her office window on the fifth floor of a building overlooking the Wilshire district, but she didn't feel like working. She hoped something would happen to justify her dereliction of duty—and, surprisingly, it did.

Distraction presented itself in the person of fashion editor Janie Frakes, a willowy African-American knockout upon whose taste the magazine depended. It was Janie who'd foreseen the coming trend toward modesty, something Belle would never have suspected, and Janie who had declared the Death of Rayon.

Carrying a coffee mug labeled I Am Woman, I Am Invincible, I Am Tired, Janie marched into Belle's office and flung herself across a velvet love seat. "You aren't going to believe what Darryl Horak is doing. I'm not sure I believe it myself. Let me ask myself this question—Janie, do you believe it? No. There, you see?"

The remaining bit of doughnut went down Belle's throat in a hard lump. "So what's he doing?"

"He's shooting next summer's centerfolds on the beach today, according to a photographer I know," Janie began.

"No doubt in front of his house," Belle grumbled. "So he can whisk the ladies into his bedroom without the inconvenience of taking them to lunch."

Janie uttered a bark of laughter. "Ooh, you do hate that man! No, actually, he lives in Redondo if I remember correctly, and they're shooting in Santa Monica. But listen! Guess who's going to be Miss May?''

Belle shrugged. She didn't pay much attention to which model was all the rage at the moment. They came and went with the speed of magazine editions.

Janie leaned toward her with the air of a spy about to impart the formula for Big Boy's secret sauce. "Constance Sasser," she said. "Is this weird? Is this unbelievable?"

Belle was outraged. "Constance Sasser?" she demanded. "*Our* Constance Sasser?"

"Apparently she whipped off her thick glasses, shed her white lab coat and bingo!" Janie said. "Darryl Horak saw her potential right in our very pages, according to the grapevine. That rat!"

"Darryl Horak reads *Just Us?*" Belle scoured every issue of *About Town,* but she was powered by pure malice. "It's—it's offensive. She's an intellectual. A scientist. A *theoretical* scientist, for Pete's sake."

A physicist at the center of controversy over her theories positing the existence of alternate universes, Constance had been the subject of a profile in *Just Us.* Belle recalled thinking that the scientist was hiding pretty blue eyes and good bone structure, but it infuriated her that Darryl Horak had noticed.

Worse, he was treating this brilliant woman like a sex object, posing her on the beach in a skimpy bathing suit for the titillation of his readers.

"What are we going to do about it?" Janie asked. "If Constance wants to take her clothes off for the masses . . . well, she's a grown woman. Grown in all the right places, I might add."

Belle didn't fully agree. Despite her brilliance, Constance was a naive young woman.

Darryl must have snowed her with his idea, once expressed in an interview Belle had read, that women were celebrating their sexuality in a healthy way by displaying their bodies for men to ogle. But, of course, only perfectly proportioned young women with great skin were allowed to celebrate their sexuality in *About Town*.

"He wants women in swimsuits?" Belle said. "Let's give him women in swimsuits!"

2

THE SHOOT WAS going perfectly.

They were tackling three Flaunt It centerfolds at once to take advantage of the still-warm September weather. Everything had dovetailed. It was a hot, sunny day and the beach lay beautifully empty. Jim Rickard, Darryl's best photographer and good buddy, had been available, and they'd lined up as stunning a trio of beauties as a man could wish for.

Technically speaking, the editor of *About Town* didn't have to be present at the shoot. Setting up the scenes was his art director's job, and Elva Ching was good at it.

But Darryl wouldn't miss the chance to be here. He wanted to insure that everything about his magazine was perfect.

After he'd graduated from college, he'd aimed for a career in show business, with the vague idea of getting into production. It hadn't taken long working as a gofer in a TV studio to discover he preferred to become his own boss as soon as possible.

He also enjoyed squiring lovely women, and helping their careers, and seeing their eyes light up with gratitude. So ten years ago, as a twenty-three-year-old, Darryl had rounded up the backing from friends and family, started the magazine out of his bachelor apartment and landed in heaven.

Somewhere during the past decade, though, the pretty women had begun blurring into one another. To his surprise, Darryl found he cared more about the editorial content and the visual quality of the magazine than about meeting yet another to-die-for model.

Then, a few years back, he'd started to get serious about one girlfriend. Celia, an attorney, was smart, independent and a knockout.

Everything had gone well until the two of them had started talking marriage. Then she'd changed.

Although Celia had maintained her own apartment, she'd begun spending most of her time at Darryl's place. She restocked his refrigerator, gave away most of his liquor and began kicking him out of bed early on weekends. He had to exercise every single day, she said, or he risked dying young.

When he'd tried to argue, Celia had produced a survey from the newspaper. It said married men depended on their wives to keep them healthy, physically and emotionally.

At that point, Darryl had no longer felt healthy in either of those departments. He'd felt trapped and stifled.

Finally, Celia herself had realized their relationship was deteriorating, and had left to try her luck elsewhere. Before departing, though, she'd warned Darryl that he needed someone to look after him.

The statement had made him angry. Men weren't overgrown kids who needed women to make them whole.

That was when Darryl's *About Town* philosophy had come into focus. As far as he was concerned, men could manage their own nutrition and exercise. They could become wine connoisseurs without losing control of their drinking. They could develop rich personal relationships with friends and family all by themselves. And his magazine would show them how.

In the past few years, he'd run a number of articles on those subjects. But Darryl didn't kid himself. Gorgeous women were still the lure that drew men to *About Town*.

Today's selection of models would certainly send pulses racing. Miss March, an aspiring actress named Mindy who had a mane of dark hair, made it clear she would enjoy having Darryl over for dinner any night he found himself free.

Next year's Miss April, with long strawberry tresses and a Cockney accent, had been unable to stop in-line skating long enough to be photographed. Finally Elva had suggested shooting her in action, and so they had. In the process, Miss April had favored Darryl with an exaggerated wink that let him know she preferred not to skate alone.

And then there was Miss May. Darryl had to congratulate himself on his coup. In addition to her physical attractions, the scientist would bring international attention to *About Town*.

The fact that he was thumbing his nose at Belle Martens in the process didn't detract from his glee one whit.

He'd tried not to think about her this past month, except as an aberration in the otherwise smooth course of his life. Okay, so she looked better than he would have expected in her birthday suit. And he couldn't erase the memory of how her breasts felt in his mouth, that mixture of firmness and yielding, those tantalizing pink nipples...

He caught himself with a jolt. He had to stop daydreaming and concentrate on business.

He forced himself to focus on Elva as she tried to sweet-talk Connie Sasser out of her shy stiffness. Their efforts would be wasted if the woman couldn't relax in front of the camera.

For Connie, Elva had chosen a green-and-silver swimsuit cut high on the hip and low in the front. The scientist, however, tended to clench her arms at her sides, as if afraid she would spill out of the thing. She also kept her head lowered, so that chin-length dark-blond hair fell over her face like a veil.

"The light's going," Jim Rickard muttered as he watched Elva try to pose Connie on a lounge chair amid an array of potted flowers. "Sun's getting harsh."

"She's worth waiting for," Darryl said.

The bearded photographer grinned at him. "Go for the intellectual type, do you?"

"I didn't mean for me, personally," he corrected. "I meant for the publicity she'll bring."

"Glad to hear you say that." Jim checked his lens filter. "You're the only guy I know smart enough to stay single into his thirties."

Jim had endured a bitter divorce the previous year. Darryl didn't pry into the gory details, but he knew Jim desperately missed his five-year-old son, Nick. It didn't seem fair that Jim's ex-wife, Tori, had taken the boy and moved to the East Coast, thus effectively denying Jim frequent visitation.

Besides, in the years Darryl had known the couple, Jim had made as many sacrifices for Nick as had Tori. Why did so many judges assume mothers were superior parents? As far as Darryl was concerned, men could take care of children just as well. Maybe one of these days he would write an article on the subject.

Elva put a tape of country music on the boom box, but Connie still didn't loosen up. "I'm sorry," the physicist said. "I don't think I can do this, after all."

"Sure you can." Elva brushed straight black bangs from her forehead, a gesture of strained patience. "You look terrific. Imagine you're alone with the man of your dreams and he's standing there admiring you, holding a glass of champagne."

"Or his Nobel Prize," Jim suggested.

"Or *your* Nobel Prize," Darryl offered.

"Or—what the hell?" said Elva.

Darryl's first impression, from the corner of his eye, was that a busload of tourists had landed. Then he realized that not only was there no bus in sight, but the new arrivals were all female and all were wearing swimsuits.

Belle Martens was leading the pack.

"I don't believe it." Jim started to laugh. "Would you look at that?"

How could I help looking at that? Darryl thought irritably.

A crowd of women, from tiny to tremendous, teenagers to senior citizens, surged toward him. Their vast variation of shapes and endowments were bared by the tiniest lot of swimsuits ever allowed to leave a store without a police escort.

Darryl counted at least twelve women. It was hard to be exact, the way they kept bouncing around. Their appearance here couldn't be a coincidence.

Nor did he believe Belle had draped her curvaceous body with a black-and-gold string bikini in the middle of a workday just to go exercise on the beach.

She probably wanted to spoil his photo shoot to get revenge for that night of passion, which he couldn't even remember. Damn it, he wanted at least the recollection of ripping the bra off those ripe breasts, and sliding a slip of fabric down her hips, and feeling her arms wrap around him as he buried himself inside—

"Oh, there's Belle!" Connie cried in relief, and jumped out of her lounge chair.

Elva threw up her hands. "There goes her concentration."

Darryl strode forward, caught Dr. Sasser by the elbow and halted her before she reached the newcomers. To Belle, he said, "Sorry, we've already hired our model."

She planted herself on the boardwalk directly in front of him. The sunlight brought out the golden highlights in her inordinately red hair and cinnamon eyes. "We're here for educational purposes."

"Really?" He eyed her bikini with deliberate provocation. "I hope you didn't pay much for that. There's hardly any material in it."

"Precisely my point." She folded her arms, which had the effect of emphasizing her cleavage. In contrast to Dr. Sasser, Belle appeared to possess no shyness whatsoever. "We want the public to see that real women come in all shapes and sizes. That you can be desirable at two hundred pounds or ninety. Big hips, small busts—who cares?"

At that moment Darryl wished that Belle did indeed weigh two hundred pounds, or better yet had opted for a hood and a large potato sack. She had no right to torment him with the body that had insisted on sneaking into his fantasies ever since their night together.

He said a silent prayer of thanks for the fact that he'd thrown a sport coat over his jeans and oxford shirt. Hopefully it was hiding his irrepressible male response.

"Where did you get this crowd, anyway?" he asked.

Belle shrugged. "My editors and I called everybody we know. The response was amazing."

"I've got a great idea." Elva Ching indicated the giggling group of visitors, who were linking arms and teaching Connie to line-dance to a song on the tape. "Let's put them all in, the way they requested."

Before Darryl could respond, Jim snatched up his camera and began shooting. "Yeah, they finally broke the ice with Dr. Sasser. This is great stuff! And get a load of that babe over there—what a trip!"

This last remark referred to a tiny woman who must have spent at least eighty summers in the sun to have achieved such a deep shade of bronze on her abundant wrinkles. A bikini hung lifelessly from her hips and chest, but the animation on her face more than compensated.

Darryl contemplated dragging Belle into the picture as well, but she stood too far away. The editor of *Just Us* clearly had no intention of appearing in an *About Town* centerfold.

A few minutes later, Jim and Elva declared themselves satisfied and began packing their equipment. The women stopped dancing and wandered off.

Belle wore the mildest expression Darryl had ever seen on her face. He might even have thought she was in a good mood, if he had not known such a thing was impossible.

"I guess we both won," she said. "You got Connie and we made our point."

"I don't plan to make a habit of breaking even," he retorted.

He expected an equally acerbic response, but Belle was frowning at something down the beach. "What do you suppose they're doing?"

Shading his eyes, Darryl made out a small TV camera crew. Across the minicam was lettered Channel 17 News. It was a station known for pursuing celebrity gossip.

The jeans-clad cameraman was following a woman in a sleek business suit, with short chestnut curls and pale predatory eyes. He recognized her as reporter Kate Munro.

Then he noticed the camera swinging toward himself and Belle. "What the hell?" he said.

"Quick!" She ducked behind him. "Shield me!"

"Why?" He tried to twist so he could see her, but she kept eluding him. How could a woman be so tiny and so forceful at the same time?

"Channel 17 is into shock news," Belle answered. "I don't know what brought them here, but the sight of me in a bathing suit will set their evil hearts dancing."

"They're probably here to get shots of Connie," said Darryl, and marched over to warn Dr. Sasser to get dressed. He couldn't help grinning at the furious noises issuing from behind him, as Belle was left without cover.

While Connie threw on her robe, he kept the reporter busy talking about how he and his staff chose their centerfolds. He never missed an opportunity to publicize his magazine. *About Town* had to compete for ads, rack space and subscribers with not only other men's magazines but also women's publications like *Just Us*.

He wondered if Channel 17 broadcast as far as the desert east of Los Angeles, where a megamall was under construction. Darryl had met with the marketing director recently about cosponsoring an "About Town" opening weekend next June.

It would be a huge splash, with celebrities, TV tie-ins, and fashion shows throughout the mall. The publicity for the *About Town* name could mean increased ads and circulation. However, the marketing director was talking with the publisher of *Just Us* as well.

That gave Darryl one more reason to monopolize the Channel 17 camera until its team finally departed. You never knew who might see the broadcast.

"It probably was Dr. Sasser they were interested in," he announced to Belle as he returned. "But they might show a few shots of you, just for comic relief."

She didn't rise to the bait. Instead, she stood with her back to him, staring at a row of newspaper vending boxes.

"What's up?" he asked.

"Excuse me?" She swung to face him, startled.

"You were looking at something."

"Nothing. The stock market."

"On the front page?"

"The Dow's up," she blurted, then called an enthusiastic farewell to her departing friends.

If there was nothing important in the papers, why did she keep standing so that she blocked his view? Darryl angled closer.

She stood her ground, waving vigorously at the group of women who were almost out of sight.

He reached toward the box on the right, which held the *Los Angeles Times*. He could read part of its headline, something about a peace conference, which he didn't think was of much interest to Belle. Or to him, either, at the moment, but he pretended great fascination.

As he peered at the headlines he leaned right over Belle, backing her body into the row of interconnected news boxes. Recoiling from the hard shapes behind her, her soft and nearly naked curves pressed against Darryl.

He discovered right then the limitations of sport coats, jeans and oxford shirts. They did nothing to lessen his instantaneous awareness that Belle was all female.

They didn't hide his masculine reaction very well, either.

"Excuse me!" she snapped. "Would you please move?"

Darryl sighed. This was not a game he could win, at least not in public. "Why don't you let me see whatever it is you're hiding?"

After a brief glare, she whirled, slammed a couple of coins into a box and jerked out a tabloid. He glimpsed the headline as it came flying out: Party Prank Leaves Dozens Dazed. Then Belle spun away, blocking his view of the paper.

"Well?" he demanded. "What does it say?"

"You can read it when I'm done!" She took a determined step forward.

Darryl, who towered at least a foot over Belle, reached over her head, plucked the newspaper from her hands and scanned the article.

"Hey!" Belle grabbed for it. "Buy your own!"

"There aren't any more." He held it out of her reach and skimmed through the details. When she stopped jumping up and down like a frustrated basketball player, he politely lowered it so she could read, too.

Darryl's body hadn't entirely forgotten her nearness, but his brain was preoccupied with absorbing the details of what had happened at the press party. It seemed that he and Belle weren't the only ones who had succumbed to the punch, which had been laced with an aphrodisiac.

Although the victims of the prank had managed to keep it quiet for weeks, eventually a waiter in search of extra income had approached the newspaper. Darryl skimmed on, then suddenly felt the air whoosh out of his chest as if someone had punched him. He handed the paper to Belle and pointed to the final paragraph.

At the same time, he heard Elva announcing her departure. She'd given Darryl a ride from the office, but he couldn't leave now. "I'll catch up with you later!" he called.

He and Belle needed to talk. Afterward, he would cadge a ride from her, since their offices were only a block apart.

She read the last sentence aloud, her voice crackling with indignation. "'Among those seen exiting together were arch-rival editors Belle Martens and Darryl Horak.' Oh, my gosh!"

"At least they don't speculate about what happened next," he offered.

"Has anyone seen this? Can we burn it? Can we smash their printing presses and shoot their staff?" she asked.

"This, from an editor?" Darryl grimaced.

"This paper is nothing but trash!"

"Well, nobody believes the garbage they run in tabloids, anyway," he said.

She let out a disgusted breath. "Channel 17 believed it. That was no coincidence, Darryl. They were after us today."

"And they got us," he observed grimly.

"Belle!" one of the women called across the sand. "You coming?"

"Go on without me!" As her friends departed, she turned back to the tabloid. "This just hit the stands today. We've got to coordinate our stories."

He nodded.

"Nothing happened," she announced.

"Absolutely nothing."

"We've hardly even met."

"We hate each other."

"Don't exaggerate," she said.

"I'm not."

Belle took a deep breath. "You know what? I'm starving. Let's go eat." Tucking the newspaper under her arm, she set off down the boardwalk so fast that Darryl had to take extralong strides to catch up.

He couldn't believe the woman's nerve. She hadn't even asked if *he* was hungry. Or maybe she realized that what he was hungry for couldn't be purchased in a restaurant.

She paused at a souvenir stand to buy a Lakers cap and a pair of cheap sunglasses. "So no one will recognize me," she said, putting them on. "Look how much trouble we're in already."

It wouldn't, of course, have occurred to her to buy a cover-up for her body, as well, he reflected ruefully.

A half block farther on, Belle led the way into a seafood shanty and ordered fried clams, garlic bread, cottage fries and milk. She paid so fast, Darryl didn't have time to reach for his wallet, which was probably a good thing, because he suspected she would have challenged him to a duel for such a chauvinist act as offering to pay.

"Milk?" Darryl said. "You drink that stuff?"

"I've got a craving." She retrieved her change and marched toward a booth in the gloom caused by smoked-glass windows, leaving him alone at the counter.

There was nothing on the menu that appealed to him: no broiled seafood, no fresh salads. Being a he-man didn't mean you had to swim in grease, a fact Darryl tried to impress upon his readers, not to mention his macho entertainment editor, Greg Ormand.

Greg didn't believe it, and the cook at this establishment obviously didn't, either. But Darryl's stomach was uttering a series of hopeful rumbles, so he ordered the house specialty of fried catfish and hush puppies and went to join Belle.

As he slipped into the booth, she folded her sunglasses and hat onto the table. "Here's the story. We left the party together. Then we went our separate ways."

"What if someone saw you leaving my house?" He ran his fingers through his precision-cut black hair. "Those tabloids pay big bucks to informers. If they find out we lied, it will be obvious why."

"I suppose so." Belle drummed bright-red nails on the tabletop. "Okay, so we went to your place and argued, and then I left."

"The next morning?"

She sighed. "Maybe nobody else will read the item. Maybe we won't have to explain this."

"Belle," said Darryl. "This is Los Angeles. We have an entire industry, of which we are a part, that feeds on meaningless trivia like this."

"What rotten luck!" She glared as if he were single-handedly responsible for their dilemma. "The first man I've... indulged myself with since my engagement broke off, and it had to be you!"

"Doesn't that tell you something?" He knew he was tempting fate, but he enjoyed watching her bosom heave with fury. Especially when it was only restrained by tiny bits of string that threatened to unravel at any moment.

"Doesn't that tell me what?" she retorted.

"You could have gone home with anyone," he said. "Subliminally, you must find me attractive."

"How do you know it wasn't *you* who selected *me*?" she returned, then fell silent as a waiter shuffled over and dumped their orders on the table.

"Would you quit staring at my chest?" Belle snapped at Darryl after the man departed. "You're making me mad on purpose."

"But you bristle so picturesquely."

"If you're not careful, I'm going to take my food and eat it somewhere else," she snarled.

"You can't do that."

"Why not?"

He stopped nibbling at his fried catfish, which tasted better than it ought to. "Because you have to give me a ride home. I came with my art director."

She paused with a forkful of clams halfway to her mouth. "But *I* came with a couple of women from the office. I was going to ask *you* for a ride."

She appeared more annoyed by this circumstance than Darryl. Indeed, his continuing exposure to Belle in her state of semiundress was making a return to the office less and less appealing.

"Let's share a cab," he said. "We'll go to my place and you can help me string my kite."

"Excuse me?"

He reached across the table, grateful for the dark seclusion of their booth, and fingered a bit of yarn poking from the side of her bikini bra. "One tug and we'll have plenty of string. But I don't suppose we'll feel like flying a kite."

"It's an old bathing suit. I happened to have it in my desk," she snapped. "If you're so in love with it, I'll have it delivered to your office."

"It won't be the same without the contents," Darryl protested.

Belle dropped her fork with a clang. "For your information, these aren't contents, this is my own personal body!"

"And a very nice half-naked one, too."

"Everybody dresses this way at the beach!"

"Besides, I know what you look like without it." He kept his voice low enough so no one else could hear. "How about a rematch?"

She choked as if too many words were fighting to escape at once.

Someone opened the restaurant door, bathing them in a burst of sunlight. Darryl leaned back, delighted by the scene before him: Belle sputtering in fury, while the bright light turned her hair and eyes into red, amber and gold fireworks.

"Don't you see, it's perfect," he teased. "We could have the ideal relationship—physical, intense and forgotten as soon as we're out of each other's sight. Maybe once a week, until we get bored. What do you say?"

He didn't know why he kept teasing her, except that it was fun, and he couldn't wait to hear what she would say next.

"Call someone to pick you up," she managed to gasp after several speechless moments. "Make sure he has a car roomy enough to accommodate your swelled head!"

With that, she clapped on her hat and sunglasses, picked up her tray and went to sit by a window.

As soon as she'd put a short distance between herself and Darryl Horak, Belle could think of a dozen rejoinders she should have made.

But she knew none of them would have erased the self-satisfied grin on his face. The arrogance of the man appalled her. How could he even suggest that she would want to come near his bedroom again?

He was obviously accustomed to females who gazed adoringly at his thick dark hair and intense eyes and lean hard body, females who agreed to everything he suggested. He deserved a woman like her, Belle reflected, someone who would stand up to him.

She wished she remembered how it had felt to make love to him. Not that she considered Darryl even moderately desirable, Belle reminded herself. She downed the last of her milk and let it ease the queasiness in her stomach.

She simply felt curious about what it had been like to sleep with him. There was nothing unnatural or demeaning in speculating about something you had experienced while in a state of unconsciousness.

Once her curiosity was satisfied, the man would never cross her mind again.

She picked up the tabloid and pretended interest in a space alien story while Darryl went to a pay phone in the corner. When he hung up and strolled toward her table, she transferred her attention to the tabloid's horoscope, which declared that she must stop letting people walk all over her.

"I called my office and yours," he said when he reached her. "They're both sending someone to pick us up."

He moved on. Two college-age girls at the next table twirled their long hair and pursed their lips in admiration as he passed. One uttered a wolf whistle.

Belle didn't know why she found their behavior so irritating.

3

ANITA RIOS, the food editor of *Just Us,* sat on the edge of Belle's desk eating a chili dog. "Nobody believes that nonsense about you and Darryl. Nobody. Not me, not this chili dog—and if you don't think it's alive, just ask my stomach."

"But has everybody seen it?" Belle demanded, rattling the tabloid. She'd spotted two copies that her staff must have picked up at lunch break.

"Well . . . yeah."

Today was definitely turning into one of *those* days. Even getting back to the office had turned out to be a battle.

When Darryl's macho entertainment editor, Greg Ormand, had showed up at the restaurant to fetch his boss, he'd failed to recognize Belle in the hat and sunglasses and had favored her with a bold stare.

Darryl had grabbed the guy's arm with unnecessary force, just as Janie Frakes had marched in to rescue Belle. Janie and Greg had recently broken off a fiery relationship, and Janie had witnessed Greg's leer. She had let him know in no uncertain terms what she thought of his adolescent need to flirt with every female he encountered.

Greg had responded with such adjectives as "controlling," "jealous," "frustrated" and "too thin." The teenagers at the next table had stared in awe at the soap opera.

On the drive back to the office with the angry Janie, Belle had found neither peace nor sympathy. And now, the tabloid had invaded her inner sanctum.

"By the way," Anita said, downing the last bite of chili dog. "What *did* happen that night?"

"With Darryl?" she asked with what she hoped was innocence. "We both fell asleep. The next morning, we woke up, took one look at each other and screamed."

That was true, as far as it went.

Anita licked her fingers. "Channel 17 called. They want to interview you about the rock party, the spiked punch and all."

"And all" meant Darryl. "Not interested," muttered Belle.

The food editor shrugged. "I've never known you to pass up an opportunity for publicity. Must be a reason, hmmm?" And off she went, brown hair curled into what looked to Belle like question marks.

The whole office must be thinking the same thing. And she had to admit, if nothing had happened, why would she turn down a chance for publicity?

She stuck her head out the door. Her secretary, Lisa, gave her a startled glance and began typing at her computer.

On Lisa's desk lay a copy of the tabloid. On the far side, craning his neck to read it, stood Tom, the gangly but efficient young man who served as traffic director. That all-important job involved shepherding editorial copy, ads, layouts, tear sheets and every other aspect of the magazine to the right people at the right time.

"Call Channel 17," Belle snapped at the secretary. "Tell them to hightail it over here. And, Tom, I'll need you in my office."

THE VOLLEYBALL GAME always started around 6:30 p.m. At quarter past six, when Darryl showed up at the beach a few blocks from his house, the usual gang of neighborhood sports enthusiasts were grouped in a huddle instead of warming up.

"What's going on?" he called, and promptly realized he should have known the answer. At the center of their semicircle rested a tiny battery-operated TV set, tuned to the Channel 17 news.

After he'd returned to the office, Darryl had been plagued by sly insinuations and open teasing about Belle Martens and their escapade. Everyone, it seemed, had either read the article or heard about it.

Now, as he approached his friends, he heard the broadcaster say, "And when we return, we'll have that item you've been waiting for—sexy editor Belle Martens talks about her alleged night of love with arch-rival Darryl Horak!"

Several faces turned guiltily toward him. Most of his friends greeted him in an offhand manner phony enough to merit a grand jury indictment.

So Belle had given an interview. Why was he not surprised? He hoped the woman would deny everything. Otherwise . . . well, otherwise he would have to retaliate.

"Hey, Darryl!" a female voice called, and the attention of everyone was instantly diverted by Miss March, brunette mane bouncing as she jogged. Mindy had swapped her swimsuit for a shrink top and microscopic shorts. Darryl wondered how she'd found him, but then, it was common knowledge that he lived in Redondo.

It might also be a coincidence, but experience had taught him that when it came to ambitious people, there were no coincidences.

"Okay! Here goes!" came a shout around him, and everyone's attention riveted on the screen.

First came a shot from the beach that afternoon. Belle could be seen ducking behind Darryl, who stood grinning foolishly. Then the picture cut to Belle's office, a stylishly decorated but cluttered room enlivened by posters of Keanu Reeves and Denzel Washington.

They hadn't run one second of his spiel about how *About Town* chose its centerfolds. This didn't bode well.

In the office, reporter Kate Munro posed beside Belle. "Now, tell me," she cooed as if they were intimate friends. "That night when you and Darryl Horak staggered out of the party together, you didn't go play Trivial Pursuit, did you?"

"Any time spent in Mr. Horak's company would have to be considered a trivial pursuit, but no." Belle's chin rose and her eyes sparkled at the camera. "We discussed circulation figures."

"You mean for your magazines?" Kate's voice dripped disbelief.

"Certainly not!" chirped Belle. "I mean our personal circulation figures. Which I'm not about to reveal, except to say that mine were a touch more spectacular than his."

With this remark, she draped her arm around someone off-camera. The camera pulled back to reveal a gangly young man squinting into the lights with an embarrassed grin.

"And this is . . . ?" said the reporter.

"My friend Tom," Belle announced. She'd changed from her swimsuit into a red sundress that plunged downward on both sides, revealing the outer edges of her breasts.

"What a babe," said one of the volleyball players.

Mindy wrinkled her nose. "I think she's tacky. Although if she offered to put me in her magazine, I wouldn't say no."

"Shhh!" said everybody else.

That fellow Tom couldn't even lift the beginner weights at the gym, Darryl sneered silently. No doubt it was an act, anyway. He was probably either the parking attendant or the janitor.

Darryl just wished Belle hadn't flung her arm around the guy's shoulder. She was so short that the gesture pressed her tight against him, and the man's grin widened until it nearly split his face.

"So you and Darryl Horak swapped war stories and one-upped each other?" probed the reporter. "Even though everyone else who drank the punch swears it induced sexual abandon?"

"Some aversions go too deep to overcome, I guess." Belle smirked.

The watchers filled the air with hoots and whistles. "Guess she put you in your place!" someone taunted.

The picture switched to the male and female co-anchors. "We're trying to reach Darryl Horak for a response," said the man. "We hope to have more for you on the nine o'clock news. And now for the weather..."

Chortling and swapping wisecracks, the volleyball players abandoned their viewing circle and headed toward the net. Mindy joined in, although she appeared more interested in watching Darryl than the ball.

He didn't enjoy her attention. He wanted to be left alone to stew about what he'd seen.

So Belle was sticking to the party line, that nothing had happened. Well and good, except that her digs about him couldn't be allowed to pass without response.

Darryl hated to lose. He particularly loathed being made to look like a jerk on television. And he had no doubt that the marketing director for the megamall would be watching this tiff with great interest.

He put in a call to the TV station from a pay phone, then returned to play a killer game of volleyball. A guy had to work off his frustrations somehow.

The sun was setting over the ocean in a smog-enhanced display of pinks and golds when the camera crew found him. Sweat soaked Darryl's black T-shirt, and he could feel the jeans clinging to every muscle in his thighs and calves.

His companions appeared equally wrung out, except for Mindy. Her only indication of a hard workout was that her shrink top appeared to have shrunk even more.

Kate Munro headed toward him, determination overwhelming her obvious distaste at the sand pouring into her pumps. Darryl paused with the volleyball under his arm, and didn't object when Mindy came to stand beside him.

He would give Belle a taste of her own medicine, he reflected. With any luck, that would be the end of the whole stupid business.

BELLE STOPPED AT a pharmacy on her way home. Her stomach had been bothering her for three days, and she'd run out of antacids.

Stalking down the aisle with a small cart, she mentally reviewed the telecast of herself, which she'd just watched at the office. Working late was par for the course, particularly when deadlines had to be met, and usually she didn't mind.

But tonight she'd felt like going home and resting. She hoped she wasn't coming down with the flu.

At least the broadcast had flattered her, according to Janie and Anita, who had also stayed late. Their only regret, voiced after Tom had departed, was that they hadn't had a more macho specimen on hand.

Oh, well, he'd enjoyed himself, and the point had been made. Belle didn't need Darryl. She could get any man she wanted.

Except that she didn't want any of them. Not since her hideously close brush with matrimony the year before. Belle's thoughts flicked back to that arch-villain of villains, her former fiancé, Fred Lowell.

At first, he'd seemed close to ideal: handsome but not flashy, steady but not dull, financially solvent and totally enamored of Belle.

His occupation as a stockbroker had further endeared him to her. She didn't want to make the mistake of marrying someone in the public eye. Too many marriages between royal egos disintegrated as careers surged.

Fred had raved about her glamour and had seemed to enjoy escorting her to fancy restaurants. He'd filled her ears with tales of the killings he'd made on the stock market for his clients and, he'd insinuated, for himself. Okay, so Belle hadn't been wildly in love with Fred, but she'd been wildly in love with the sense of security he brought.

Until the day federal agents had marched him off to face charges of fraud. And selling stocks without a license. And misrepresentation and breach of trust and a bunch of other allegations.

Fred Lowell turned out to be a con man who was participating in the witness protection program after testifying against a drug dealer. He had made the feds look like idiots and Belle feel like a fool, and he got convicted to the tune of a long prison sentence.

The only blessing was that they hadn't publicly announced the engagement, so she'd been spared the full glare of the news cameras. To the reporters who'd phoned, she had described Fred as a business acquaintance who'd been advising her on investments.

Fortunately, she hadn't made any. On her salary, she couldn't afford to.

Belle left the pharmacy with only the vaguest idea of what she'd purchased. She was a disorganized shopper who rarely made lists, and tonight she'd gone down the aisles and through the checkout in a weary and preoccupied daze.

Well, if she'd bought anything she didn't need, she would donate it to charity.

As she picked up a couple of cartons of Chinese food a block from home, Belle reminded herself that she'd sworn to go on a diet. But she couldn't handle one tonight. Not when the newscasters had promised to air Darryl's rebuttal on the nine o'clock news.

As she pulled into the carport of her condo, in a small development tucked among the houses and apartments of the Palms area, she checked her watch. Half an hour to go.

She was unlocking the front door when her neighbor, Moira McGregor, poked her head out.

"That was fun today." Moira was the high-spirited octogenarian who had been among the swimsuit participants. "Which issue will the picture be in?"

"Next May." Belle propped the door open, sacks clutched in her arms. "Thanks for coming."

"I saw you on the news," said her neighbor. "I don't care what anybody says, I hope you banged that man's brains out. He's a good looker, even if he is stuck on himself, and you deserve a little fun." With that startling remark, the old gray head disappeared into the condo.

Belle staggered into her living room and dropped the pharmacy sacks on the coffee table. One flopped onto its side and the contents spilled out, giving her a clear view of what she'd purchased.

Now why had she bought sunscreen with a protection factor of fifteen when she meant to get twenty-five? And she didn't need conditioner, she needed mousse.

Most perplexing, how could she have thrown in a pregnancy test when she'd been reaching for the manicure set right next to it?

With a grimace of disgust, Belle carted her Chinese food into the dining area.

As she downed the aromatic shrimp and beef with broccoli, she reflected that she ought to finish decorating the condo. She'd purchased it three years ago, only to watch real estate prices plummet in Southern California.

Since Belle hadn't intended to sell the place in the near future, the decline in value of her condo had had no immediate effect except to make her feel poor. Therefore, instead of consulting an interior designer, she'd relied on her own taste in picking up a few items here and there.

Unfortunately, she tended to fall in love with individual objects without considering how they fit into the overall scheme. As a result, a Regency sofa reigned over a modern brass-and-glass coffee table and a huge Oriental vase full of dried pampas grass.

Belle had failed to pull the whole thing together, and had even worsened the effect by adding an inexpensive Persian carpet and an armoire picked at a garage sale in Beverly Hills. And her ever-expanding collection of books was crammed into makeshift shelves supported by cinder blocks.

Maybe she should spray-paint everything red. That might do the trick.

The food helped settle Belle's stomach. She ought to start a load of laundry; she ought to open her mail; she ought to pay some bills. But the same sense of exhaustion that had dogged her for days kept her rooted to the chair.

Wondering why her feet had begun to swell, she kicked off her shoes and groped behind her on the sideboard until she found the remote control.

She clicked to the news, which appeared on the oversize TV set positioned across the living room. The headline items were footage of two politicians shaking hands over a treaty, and a government expert announcing that the economy was finally booming, or it was crashing, or it was leveling off, depending on which set of statistics you used.

The anchorpersons returned. "Earlier, you saw our interview with Belle Martens, who edits the women's magazine *Just Us,*" said the female half of the duo. "Witnesses claim that she and rival editor Darryl Horak drank spiked punch and landed in bed together."

"We promised to get a response from the man himself," said her male counterpart. "Belle denies the claim, but does he? Here's Kate Munro with Darryl Horak's side of the story."

The scene switched to a beach at sunset. There stood Darryl, dark hair finger-combed away from his forehead, sweaty T-shirt clinging to his muscular chest, a volleyball under one arm. The picture of virility.

"Does Belle Martens ring *my* bell? I'm too much of a gentleman to say." His cocky grin made her itch to tell him what she thought of his claim to good manners. "But you know, in my position, I'm surrounded by gorgeous ladies. One more or less would hardly be noticed."

From off-camera, he pulled a woman, her camera-ready smile glittering with perfect teeth. The other volleyball players visible in the background ogled her abundant dark hair and "Baywatch" figure.

Mercifully, the camera cut to Kate Munro. "People say that opposites attract. Now tell the truth, Mr. Horak. Belle Martens has gone home with you, and there she is lying on your bed zonked out of her mind. Can you honestly say you wouldn't take advantage of the situation?"

"I'd cover her with the biggest blanket I could find and check into a hotel," Darryl responded, to the laughter of his friends.

"Thank you, Darryl Horak." The reporter stared directly out from the screen. "Now back to the studio."

The co-anchors returned. "I think we'd have to term those two a real odd couple," said the woman.

You're not kidding, Belle snarled silently, and switched off the set. She felt like calling the station to report that, far from covering her with a blanket, Darryl had leered at her that very afternoon and proposed a rematch.

Great idea, Belle. Why don't you go stick your finger in a light socket next?

She had known she was upset but she hadn't realized how upset until she felt her entire Chinese dinner begin an upward march through her esophagus. Choking it back, Belle raced for the bathroom.

A few miserable minutes later she emerged, aware for the first time that her stomach troubles meant more than just mild indigestion.

She'd been nauseated on and off for days. Her feet hurt and her energy hovered near zero. When she'd put on her bikini today, she'd noticed that her breasts were swollen, but had attributed it to a general weight gain.

Belle's calendar wouldn't be much help because she never kept track of things. She had to rely on her memory, which said that she'd begun her most recent period the day of Janie's twenty-eighth birthday party.

That had been the last day of July. Six weeks ago.

She was two weeks late. She was nauseated. And for some subconscious reason, she'd thrown a pregnancy test into her cart.

Grimly, she took the test and marched back into the bathroom. The directions told her to wait until first thing in the morning, but she never paid attention to details like that.

It wouldn't have mattered, anyway. The tube turned blue as the sky, blue as Lake Tahoe, blue as the white underwear Belle had washed with a navy sweater.

She sank onto the Regency couch and thumped her feet onto the brass-and-glass coffee table. Of all the impossible, unforeseen, dreadful things Darryl Horak could have done to her, this one deserved a prize.

It was horribly unfair. She couldn't even remember having fun.

Hands clenched in her lap, Belle gave herself a pep talk.

It isn't that bad. Maybe it's a blessing in disguise. You're thirty-one and you've always wanted kids. This way you don't have to marry some creep to get them.

She thought about her four-year-old niece, Mikki. Usually the child was a blazing bundle of energy, but once when Belle had put her to bed, she'd nestled close like a kitten.

Belle remembered the warm feel of the girl, and the sight of that sweet face softening into slumber. Raising a child might be difficult at times, but she wanted that challenge and the rewards that came with it. This pregnancy might be unexpected, but it wasn't unwelcome.

The one thing she didn't want was any further involvement with Darryl Horak. She must figure out a way to present her pregnancy so no one would suspect what had happened.

Lots of women got artificially inseminated, didn't they? So why not claim that she had, too?

Even if he suspected the truth, Darryl would probably steer clear. He might have planted his seed inside Belle, but if she got her way, that would be the last thing he would ever have to do with this baby.

4

"THAT MARKETING DIRECTOR should be here any minute." Janie Frakes peered toward the restaurant door. "Are you tense? Do you have butterflies in your stomach?"

"I have a great void in my stomach," muttered Belle, reaching for another piece of bread. She caught Janie's disapproving frown, but the fashion editor kept silent.

Everyone had noticed how Belle was gaining weight. She'd sworn to keep her secret as long as possible, intending to be one of those women so svelte that no one realizes they're pregnant until they give birth to triplets. But her appetite, in combination with a queasy stomach, defied her.

Today, she didn't care about her burgeoning figure. She was more concerned about gaining the good opinion of Mira Lemos, the marketing director of the future High Desert Megamall.

If Mira chose *Just Us* to cosponsor the mall's opening weekend, it would be a major coup for the magazine. It would mean more ads, more publicity, more subscribers and more prestige.

With Mira's busy schedule, it had taken weeks to arrange this lunch. Its vital purpose was to promote a "Just Us" theme for the opening weekend.

The mall's grand unveiling would take place in June. Since it was only early November, under ordinary circumstances that would leave plenty of time for Belle to organize her plans.

But the way pregnancy was sending her body into new and unexplored realms of discomfort, she wasn't sure she'd be able to prepare for the opening unless she got a big head start. Doggone Darryl Horak and his over-achieving sperm!

Since September, Belle had only seen his arrogant self twice, at press parties. Both times she had glimpsed him across a crowded room, in the company of gorgeous women. His air of virulent self-confidence had made her stomach churn. But then, it didn't take much to make her stomach churn these days.

She twisted in her seat and gave the door another glance. The trendy Beverly Hills eatery was crowded to-day, its outdoor terraces packed with the well-dressed and the dying-to-be-seen. She hoped Mira wouldn't have any trouble finding them.

Across the table, Janie reached into a portfolio and pulled out her notes. "Okay, so we're going to emphasize that 'Just Us' is a terrific theme because it sounds cozy. And the mall needs to cultivate that image because it's so huge and impersonal. Belle? Are you listening?"

"Sure." Actually, she had been trying to remember whether her ultrasound was scheduled for tomorrow or the following day. The way she was gaining weight, the doctor wanted to make sure everything was progressing normally.

Normal? A child fathered by Darryl Horak? Belle would be relieved if the kid didn't have horns and a tail.

"I wish the pink ghost were here," Janie muttered, stowing away her notes. "For moral support, if nothing else. What do you suppose she has to do today that's more important? This magazine is her baby and she should give it more tender loving care."

"The pink ghost" referred to Sandra Duval, publisher and owner of *Just Us* magazine. Pink stood for the color she preferred for her stylish and very expensive clothes. Her staffers called her a ghost because she was seldom seen.

At eighteen, Sandra had been Belle's roommate at Cal State Fullerton, also majoring in communications. At twenty she'd fallen in love and had left college to marry a multimillionaire three times her age. Widowed at twenty-five, she had purchased a struggling women's magazine called *You and Me.*

Sandra's two major contributions had been to rename it *Just Us* and to hire her old roommate as editor. For the past six years, she had left almost everything to Belle.

But it never hurt to have the glamorous pink ghost, known for her extravagant parties and movie star escorts, show up to impress a potential advertiser. Sandra always managed to be charming, even if she did give the impression of having just blown in from another planet.

"I haven't seen her in weeks," Belle said. "I left an e-mail message on her computer but... Oh, no. Tell me it isn't true."

Janie followed her gaze. "Ugh. Please tell *me* it isn't true."

In rapt conversation with the maître d' stood Darryl Horak. From the tilt of his chin above the Italian leather jacket to the precise angle at which he braced his cashmere-encased legs, he was every inch a man about town.

Beside him stood the slightly taller figure of his entertainment editor, Greg Ormand. Less of a clotheshorse, he wore a russet turtleneck sweater whose chief asset was to reveal every carefully cultivated muscle in his chest and shoulders. He gave new definition to the phrase "Flaunt It."

"The man has no class," growled Janie, who still hadn't forgiven her ex-boyfriend for slighting her. "At least yours wears decent clothes."

"Mine?" returned Belle. "Are you referring to Darryl Horak as mine?"

Janie bit her lip. The subject of that drugged night together had been mercifully allowed to die, except for occasional joking references on Channel 17.

"I certainly hope they don't see Ms. Lemos before we do," Janie said. "They'd steal her in a minute. Does Greg have morals? No, he does not!"

"Let's go stand in the doorway so we can spot her first," said Belle.

"You mean . . . *near* those two?" said Janie.

"We'll eclipse them." Belle stood, then wished she hadn't. Her center of gravity had slipped to somewhere around her knees, and she had to grip the back of the chair for support.

"I'm going to save our seats." The fashion editor remained planted in her chair. "It's so crowded in here, the waiters have been eyeing our table like jackals."

No way was Belle going out there alone. She reached down, seized Janie's portfolio and slammed it onto the center of the table, barely missing their water glasses. "They won't give our table away *now*," she said. "Come on."

As they neared the restaurant's entrance, Darryl's head swiveled toward them, and one eyebrow arched in the perfect delineation of mocking curiosity. "Ladies, what brings you here?"

"We're watching for someone," Belle announced, stationing herself as far from him as possible while she scanned the restaurant's outdoor terraces below.

"Hello, Janie." Greg eyed the fashion editor with appreciation. "Your hair looks cool."

Janie fingered her coiled braids. "Just a little something I threw together."

Belle, who had heard Janie cursing about the hours it took to fix her braids, struggled to keep a straight face. She couldn't understand how an otherwise rational woman could behave so foolishly around a man.

"Why don't you fellows go and sit down?" she asked. "*You* aren't looking for someone, are you?"

"We're waiting for a table," Darryl said. "Mind if we share yours?"

"Sorry. We won't have any spare seats when—" Belle stopped as Janie grabbed her arm.

Sunshine gleamed off Mira Lemos's raven hair as she made her way up the terraces. In her suit and pumps, the marketing director formed a picture of crisp professionalism.

"Go on!" Belle gave Darryl a shove. "Take our table! We'll wait!"

But his eye had fallen on Mira, as well. "Don't be silly. We'd be happy to join you. I'm sure Ms. Lemos wouldn't mind."

As the marketing director came through the door, Belle made a feeble attempt to divert the woman's attention. "I'd like you to meet my fashion editor, Janie Frakes," she blurted. "Why don't we go sit—"

"And of course you remember me." Darryl favored the woman with a dazzling smile.

To Belle's dismay, Mira wouldn't hear of banishing Darryl and Greg. The more, the merrier, she insisted.

It was hard not to grumble as the men rearranged the plates and swiped vacant chairs from nearby tables. Those big masculine bodies crowded Belle and Janie, but left extra room for Mira.

However, Belle knew better than to make a fuss. Sometimes a person had to accept defeat gracefully, and then watch for any way to turn it into a victory.

They made small talk through the antipasto. Once their meals arrived—fettuccine for Belle and Greg, salad for everyone else—Mira asked about their preliminary ideas.

Glancing at Belle for approval, Janie said, "We'd like to focus on coziness and intimacy. A 'Just Us' theme could help humanize the mall."

"That's a good idea." Mira made a note.

"I'd say you need a larger idea to match your grand scale," Darryl interjected. " 'Just Us' makes me think of linens, tableware and lingerie. Whereas 'About Town' includes the whole range of shops, not to mention the Cineplex and the restaurants."

"It has a more sophisticated connotation," added Greg.

"This is the age of the family," countered Belle. "Commitment is in style. 'Just Us' connotes nesting and homebuilding."

"I like that." Mira made another note.

From the grim set of his jaw, Darryl wasn't about to concede the advantage. "And men can't build families?" he challenged. "Men can't maintain intimacy? Haven't you heard how many dads are becoming single fathers, and doing it successfully?"

"A tiny minority," Belle objected. "Then they complain and play on everyone's sympathy."

"Interesting points," said Mira. "Sometimes an interchange like this is more productive than meeting with people separately. It generates creativity."

Belle didn't consider today's meeting productive. In fact, her whole presentation had somehow gotten lost in the squabbling between her and Darryl.

Then, glancing out the window, she saw the one person who could rescue them. The pink ghost, blond hair squiggling loose from her chrysanthemum-trimmed hat, sauntered up the terraces waving and smiling like Carol Channing making an entrance in *Hello Dolly*.

People waved, eager to catch the eye of the city's pre-eminent arts patron and hostess. The maître d' scurried forward solicitously, and Sandra accepted his welcome with a gracious tilt of the head.

Perfume wafted from her fluttering hands and every eye in the room fixed on the layers of hand-painted silk adorning her slim frame as Sandra advanced across the room. There were hundreds of actresses in Los Angeles and dozens of socialites, but only one Sandra Duval.

Belle jumped up to greet her. The sudden movement made her feel lumpish and wrinkled, and she smoothed down her smock. She could feel Darryl's gaze rake her body, and hoped he hadn't noticed her weight gain.

Halfway across the room, Sandra stopped to chat with an acquaintance. Belle was about to go shanghai her boss when a waiter with the world's worst timing pushed up a dessert cart and halted, blocking her path.

"We don't want anything, thank you," she said.

"We have a wonderful cherry cheesecake today," the man announced as if he hadn't heard. "And have you tried our chocolate raspberry torte?"

"Didn't you hear the lady?" snapped Darryl. "If she says she doesn't want dessert, you shouldn't tempt her."

"Sorry, sir." The waiter angled the cart away.

Belle glanced at Darryl with a trace of annoyance. "Thanks for the help, but I can handle temptation all by myself."

His glance flew to her waist. "You used to have a ter-rific figure."

She knew she ought to ignore the remark, but she couldn't. Maybe it was a hormonal surge, but these days she found it almost impossible not to lash out when pro-voked. "Why don't you come right out and say I've been overeating? Isn't that what you mean?"

"Overeating?" Sandra arrived at the table like the *Queen Elizabeth II* cruising into New York Harbor. She spread her arms in a gesture of delight. "Why, just look at the woman. This increasing girth is not the result of morsels passing her lips, I assure you!"

Sandra Duval might appear to have a heart and mind of fuzz with her displays of imperious frivolity, but, as Belle recalled from their student days, she was a sharp observer. Sandra often saw clearly what everyone else missed.

Before Belle could signal or do anything more than stand there with a sinking sensation, she heard her employer proclaim, "How could you possibly think Belle is fat? Where are your eyes? Anyone can see the girl is pregnant!"

DARRYL SANK INTO the chair in his office, feeling as if he had been thumped on the head by a dozen volleyballs in rapid succession.

Belle Martens was pregnant. That was one possibility that had never occurred to him. For a sophisticated man about town, he had sauntered through the past few months like an ignorant schoolboy.

At first, as he'd sat in stunned silence at the table, he had been willing to believe her proclamation that she'd had artificial insemination. Why not? Everyone else had bought it.

Okay, maybe that fashion editor had regarded him with a flash of disgust, but he might have misinterpreted. It was the kind of gaze Janie Frakes usually reserved for Greg, and it was possible Darryl had intercepted it by mistake.

Certainly Sandra Duval hadn't batted an eye. Well, that wasn't quite true. Actually, she'd batted her eyes frequently, showing off long lashes that had probably once graced the butt end of a mink. But certainly she hadn't questioned the provenance of Belle's baby.

Baby. The word clanged through his head like a bell. The End of Your Liberty bell.

On the desk, Darryl's phone rang and he let the machine answer it. It was a free-lance writer calling to pitch him story ideas. He couldn't deal with routine matters, not now.

He made a bleary assessment of his office. The building had needed a face-lift when he'd purchased it three years ago. It still did. Beneath the old movie posters, the paint was peeling. The entire Roman Empire could have suffered lead poisoning and died from his windowsill alone.

It had seemed like a good idea to buy *About Town* its own offices. And what a steal it had seemed when, in the middle of a recession, a building had come on sale at a reasonable price right on Wilshire Boulevard.

Darryl had admired the open courtyard in the center and the balconies running around each floor. But the most attractive part of the deal had been the fact that the first level was occupied by shops.

With the rental income, he managed to make the payments. But there were never enough profits to make the planned renovations, and he was tired of working in a dump.

He needed to put all his energy into boosting circulation, winning this contract with the High Desert Megamall and promoting his publication. What he didn't need was a baby or a wife.

Wife. There was another headache-inspiring word, especially when it came attached to the person of Belle Martens.

Darryl was willing to admit he found the woman attractive. Even during their hottest arguments, sometimes she got a light in her eyes that made him want to stop battling and kiss her.

But marriage? It would be like that debacle with Celia, only ten times worse. Belle was feistier and bossier than his former girlfriend. They would quarrel over every detail of Darryl's life-style, and the only way to get peace would be to surrender.

He couldn't live that way. The very thought of having a woman run his life made his chest feel heavy and his throat clamp shut.

Darryl forced himself to take a deep breath. He was being irrational.

After all, Belle had insisted she'd gotten pregnant through the miracle of modern science. If that's what she wanted to claim, who was he to interfere?

Trying to ignore the doubts nagging at his gut, he picked up his phone to return the free-lancer's call.

He spent most of the afternoon editing copy and going over the countdown, a one-page list of stories for the February issue. "In Spring, a Man's Fancy Turns to Sports" was the theme.

Elva Ching wandered in to discuss her ideas for illustrating the issue. As she talked, Darryl mused that she was a lot like him. Fiftyish and divorced, Elva seemed to enjoy living alone. A talented painter, she liked the freedom to work at any hour and make as big a mess as she pleased.

After approving her ideas, he said, "Do you ever have any regrets? I realize this is getting personal, but I mean about being divorced with no kids?"

"It's better than being divorced *with* kids," she zinged back. "Are you serious?"

"Just doing a little thinking." Seeing her dubious expression, it occurred to Darryl that he ought to provide some excuse, so he added, "It must be because of Thanksgiving coming up in three weeks."

"Just ignore it," said Elva.

"I do kind of miss not having a family for the holidays." Darryl's father had died a few years ago. His mother, Susan, had remarried and lived in France, where her husband worked for a multinational corporation.

"Families weigh you down with expectations," advised his art director.

"You're really into this single business, aren't you?" he said.

"No more than you are." She regarded him askance. "Greg told me what happened at lunch. The kid's yours, isn't it?"

"Did Greg say that?"

Elva's straight black hair swung as she shook her head. "No. He buys the business about artificial insemination. I think it's one heck of a coincidence, in view of the timing."

"Well," Darryl said, "as a hardheaded, career-minded woman, what do *you* think I should do?"

"The woman wants you out of her life," Elva said. "So stay out."

"What about the baby?" Darryl couldn't help asking. "Won't he miss having a father?"

"*She* will probably be born with a bush of red hair and a mouth full of smart remarks," Elva remarked. "Besides, if Belle Martens needed help, she'd ask for it."

He doubted that Belle would ask him for help, under any circumstances. But Elva was right. Belle knew her own mind and besides, she was the mother. She came equipped with the right physical and mental instincts for parenthood, whereas he...

...whereas he was just like that judge who had assumed Jim's ex-wife must be the better parent, Darryl realized.

"You've got the strangest expression on your face," Elva said.

"I was thinking about Jim," he admitted. "His son needs him."

"That's different," she said. "They were married and they lived together. Nick got used to having his daddy around."

"So you think mothers are biologically better suited to be parents?" Darryl challenged.

The art director gave him a wry grin. "You're not dragging me into an argument. But most people would see it that way, I suppose."

"What if most people are wrong?" Darryl pictured a wistful little boy with a catcher's mitt in one hand and a baseball in the other, glumly staring out the window while his mother tried to persuade him to take dancing lessons.

A boy needed a father. If it was a boy, of course.

He remembered something from the conversation at the restaurant. Mira had asked Belle about the sex of the baby and she'd mentioned having an ultrasound scheduled for today or tomorrow.

It seemed important to him to learn the child's gender. If he asked Belle about the ultrasound, though, she would tell him it was none of his business.

"By the way," he said as Elva got up to leave. "Are there any good obstetricians around here?"

"Obstetricians?" she asked.

"Someone with an office close by, or else a celebrity doctor, you know, the kind movie stars go to." He was willing to bet that Belle had either chosen someone near her building for pure convenience, or else a big shot in Beverly Hills.

"I'll do some research and let you know." Elva went out shaking her head.

He felt a moment's doubt as she vanished. What had he set in motion?

An image of Jim and Nick came into his mind, the last time he'd seen the two of them together. They'd been building a sand castle on the beach, faces puckered in identical expressions of concentration.

Darryl had never given much thought to children, but now he found himself fascinated by the idea of having a son. Maybe men, too, had a biological clock. If he ever got around to writing an article about Jim, he'd have to work that subject in, too.

His digital watch had just clicked to 1635 hours when the art director returned and dropped a short list on his desk.

"There's a Dr. Marsteller in Beverly Hills, very big with the celebs. A Dr. Cohen downstairs in Belle's building. And a Dr. Friedberg in the Palms area. If I'm not mistaken, that's where she lives. But I doubt they'll tell you anything over the phone."

"We'll see," said Darryl. "Thanks a million. This is great."

He picked up the handset and waited until Elva left before he dialed. A twinge of guilt reminded him that he was prying into Belle's affairs, but he brushed it aside. He just wanted to know the results of the ultrasound, that was all.

When Dr. Marsteller's receptionist answered the phone, Darryl said, "My wife was scheduled for an ultrasound. I can't seem to get hold of her and I was wondering if I could check on the results."

"Your wife's name?" said the woman.

"Belle Martens."

He heard the click of a computer and then she said, "We don't have a patient by that name."

"I'm sorry, I must have the wrong doctor." Darryl hung up quickly.

What if Belle was using a pseudonym? But she couldn't do that because the insurance would be in her name, he reminded himself.

Dr. Cohen's line was busy. Dr. Friedberg didn't have a patient named Martens, either.

Finally Darryl got through to Dr. Cohen's office, the one in Belle's office building. He listened to the same clicking noises, then the receptionist said, "We don't have a Belle, but we do have a B. Felicia Martens."

Darryl decided to take a chance. "Yes, that's her."

"She isn't scheduled until two o'clock tomorrow afternoon," the receptionist said. "Would you like to attend? We welcome fathers."

Certainly they welcomed fathers. This was the end of the twentieth century, an enlightened time when dads were just as important as moms, Darryl told himself. Or they ought to be, if it weren't for small-minded judges.

Besides, Belle would turn five shades of purple if he showed up. Just thinking about it made him chuckle.

"Of course I'll be there," he said. "I wouldn't miss it for the world."

5

IN THE LADIES' ROOM one floor below the *Just Us* offices, Belle finished putting on her disguise and examined herself in the mirror.

One Pucci scarf—check.

One pair of sunglasses—check.

One application of pale pink lipstick, the kind she wouldn't be caught dead in—check.

No one would recognize her now. Or at least, they couldn't be sure it was her.

If only she didn't look so lumpy. Day by day, she grew more puffy and uncomfortable. Weren't pregnant women supposed to glow?

Belle had never witnessed the stages of pregnancy in anyone. None of her friends had children. Her sister, Bari, had a little girl, but they lived in Maryland.

She had expected a few moments of nausea in the morning, following by days filled with sunshine and roses. No one had prepared her for vitamins that resembled horse pills, doctor's visits where she was prodded and poked, and the fact that the smell of coffee made her feel like Jabba the Hutt on a bad day.

At least she had been given to believe that ultrasounds didn't hurt, Belle reflected as she started toward the elevator, then changed her mind and took the stairs. She needed the exercise. Besides, she was less likely to encounter anyone she knew there.

It was certainly convenient having an obstetrician in the building. She had been able to duck in there and pass it off as a long lunch break, although that was no longer necessary now that her co-workers knew of her condition.

Emerging on the lower floor, Belle stifled a moment of anxiety. The doctor had been concerned about her rapid weight gain. Could there be something wrong?

She hadn't felt the baby move yet. In fact, she'd been trying not to think about the fact that she was carrying an actual small future human being, the kind that repays years of loving sacrifice by borrowing the car without permission and taking his friends joyriding through the Mojave Desert.

Maybe, she reflected as she pushed open the office door, she should consider giving it up for adoption. The trouble was, what kind of woman would go through artificial insemination and then put the baby up for adoption?

If she'd been thinking clearly, she could have claimed she was a surrogate mother. That would have made for a terrific series of first-person articles in *Just Us*. Belle had always wanted to write fiction.

On hearing her name, the receptionist said, "Oh, yes, Mrs. Martens, you're right on time! Do you want us to wait for your husband?"

She didn't bother to tell the woman she had no husband. "No, thank you."

"I'll buzz the nurse, then."

An efficient vision in white emerged a moment later, escorted Belle to a cubicle and handed her a hospital gown to wear. Alone behind a skimpy curtain, Belle removed her peasant blouse and full skirt. The elastic already felt tight around her expanding midsection.

The nurse came back a few minutes later. "The technician is ready for you, Mrs. Martens, and your husband is here."

"I don't think so." Belle wondered if this was somebody's idea of a joke. Had Janie dressed up in a man's suit and put on a fake mustache?

"Oh, yes," the woman said as they walked down a short hall. "He called yesterday and specifically asked to be here."

Obviously, there had been a mistake; probably the doctor had two women patients with similar names. Belle braced herself for the inevitable embarrassment that such a mix-up would cause.

She was about to march into a tiny room, wearing nothing but sunglasses and a puny garment that could easily double as a cleaning rag, and find herself face-to-face with a startled and completely unfamiliar man.

She wondered if he was cute. She might let him watch.

The ultrasound room had its lights turned low, and a curtain surrounded the equipment. When she entered, Belle felt as if she were strolling into the haunted house at a Halloween party, except that she was the only one wearing a costume.

She prepared an apologetic smile as the nurse led her around the curtain. "Gee, I guess there's been a mis..."

There was no point in finishing the sentence, because there had been no mistake. Or rather, there had been a huge, enormous, pigheaded one.

DARRYL COULDN'T BELIEVE the woman was wearing sunglasses to an ultrasound. Who was she planning to fool?

Besides, the paraphernalia prevented him from getting a good look at her shocked expression, which spoiled a lot of the fun. He'd had a hard time falling asleep last night for all the chortling as he imagined Belle's reaction today.

"Hi, honey," he said.

The technician, indifferent to the vibes thrumming across the room, instructed her to lie on a padded table.

Belle made quite a production of climbing onto the padded table and flopping down on her back.

"This might feel a little cool." The technician parted the front of the gown and squirted some goo on Belle's stomach, then took a device that resembled a computer mouse and moved it across her stomach.

Darryl's gaze shifted to the ultrasound screen. All he could see was a gray blur. He might as well have been looking at a close-up look of Belle's kidneys.

"Okay, I think we're getting an arm here," said the technician. "And there's the heartbeat." She pointed at something pulsating in the middle of the screen.

"It's kind of rapid, isn't it?" Darryl asked.

"Babies' hearts beat faster than adults'," said Belle, removing her sunglasses.

Did women know these things by instinct? He refused to believe it. "Did you read about that somewhere?"

"My doctor showed me," she said. "We could hear the heartbeat on his stethoscope."

To Darryl's surprise, it bothered him that he'd missed that experience. By the time he'd even learned of the baby's existence, a significant milestone in its life had already passed.

On the screen, the picture coalesced into a baby. A lump formed in Darryl's throat. The kid was tiny, but it possessed a nose, feet, hands, even fingers. Incredible.

"He's sucking his thumb." The technician pointed. "See there?"

"'He,'" Darryl repeated. "It's a boy?"

"Let's see if we can tell." The technician swooped her mouse over Belle's stomach.

"What do you mean, 'if'?" he demanded.

"Sometimes you can tell, sometimes not," the woman explained. "There, that looks like a penis—nope, just a shadow."

"Try harder, will you?" Darryl had come here expecting to learn the child's sex. What good was modern science if it couldn't determine that?

"Who cares?" said Belle.

He shrugged. "You need to know what color to paint the nursery, don't you?"

"I'm painting it purple," she said.

The technician shook her head. "I'm afraid Baby's not going to cooperate. Are you having an amniocentesis? You can find out that way."

"Of course she is." Darryl wanted answers and he didn't want to wait six months for them.

"Only if you let them stick a needle in *your* abdomen while you're wide-awake, too," Belle snapped.

"They don't really do that," he said. "Do they?"

"All the time," said the technician.

Darryl's stomach gave a reflexive quiver at the thought of being jabbed with a needle. It probably felt different for women, though. Maybe they had fewer nerve endings in the abdomen, kind of a protective evolutionary development. Although he didn't think amniocenteses had been around long enough to have spurred evolutionary changes.

"Your husband seems anxious about the sex," observed the technician as she pressed a button and took a picture of the screen image.

"He wants a boy," Belle said. "So he can flaunt it." She emphasized the last two words.

"I do not!" The accusation stung, primarily because it was true. Or was it? Darryl had never considered what it would be like to have a daughter.

He studied the screen again as the technician moved her mouse, seeking another angle for the next picture. Someday that squiggly creature would be a beautiful bride, marching down the aisle. Or a big strong man, playing high school football as Darryl had done. Or, since Belle was the mother, it might turn out to be a short, feisty woman barreling down the football field, bowling men over left and right.

A girl would need a father to warn her about the tricks boys used to get what they wanted. And to reassure her about her own desirability. And to make it clear that not all members of the male sex were the enemy.

Fathers were important to their children of both sexes, he reflected. And surely the relationship began even before birth.

Darryl remembered his idea about writing an article on men's biological instincts and their equal importance as parents. Better yet, in personal journalism, it sometimes paid to exaggerate for effect. Suppose he claimed to believe in the natural superiority of men as parents, even during pregnancy?

What a storm of controversy that would provoke! It would give the circulation of *About Town* a real boost, and it could force readers to rethink their assumptions. It might even influence a few judges, whom he suspected enjoyed the Flaunt It centerfolds as much as the next man.

Best of all, Darryl thought, he could do the research and help Belle at the same time. It was a perfect opportunity.

AS SHE CHANGED into her clothes, Belle gave her stomach another wipe with the tissue. That stuff wasn't coming off; it would have to soak in. She didn't mind the indignity of the procedure so much as the fact that Darryl had stood there watching the whole thing.

The nerve of that man, showing up today! What had been his point, anyway? He couldn't expect her to believe he was actually interested in the child.

He'd come to gloat, that was it. He'd come to vaunt the fact that he still had his hard, sleek figure, while she was ballooning.

At least the ultrasound had proved that the pregnancy was normal, that the excess weight was the result of maybe a touch of overeating. The baby looked fine.

Belle glanced at the picture the technician had given her for the baby's scrapbook. That tiny bundle had such a cute, curvy shape. Well, if Darryl expected her to thank him, he could wait until they made frozen daiquiris in hell.

When she emerged a few minutes later and didn't see him, she told herself the worst was over. She would march through this pregnancy just fine without Mr. Fair-weather Friend.

Then she saw Darryl waiting in the outer office. She gritted her teeth as he exited the doctor's office beside her, and hoped he would quickly be on his way.

Instead, as soon as they were alone, Darryl said, "I've got an idea."

"Maybe we should discuss this some other time," she said. "In private." Suppose one of her colleagues saw them together and drew the obvious conclusion about the baby's paternity?

"I have no problem with discussing it now." His dark, rather saturnine face pressed close to hers. "I'll whisper in your ear, if you like."

She didn't like. His nearness was having a disturbing effect on her nerve endings, raising bursts of static like an electrical storm.

"Maybe there's an empty office around." Hurrying away, Belle tried a couple of unmarked doors until one opened. Switching on a light, she stepped inside.

And found herself in a storage closet. Between the walls of shelving holding cleaning supplies and wrapped paper products, there was just enough room for two people to crowd inside, if they were on very, very good terms.

Which she and Darryl were not. But it was too late. He had followed her inside and closed the door. "Very nice," he said.

With his broad shoulders looming over her and his hips only inches from hers and the tight space magnifying the scent of his after-shave, Belle kept flashing back to that morning when she'd awakened in his bed. What *had* it felt like when they'd made love?

"So what's your idea?" she said.

"I feel responsible for this," he began.

"You *are* responsible."

"Half responsible," he said.

She wanted to argue, but as a modern woman, she couldn't. "You're offering to contribute to my expenses?"

"Expenses?"

"Insurance doesn't cover everything," she responded.

This obviously wasn't what he'd expected. Darryl's jaw worked for a moment before he said, "Naturally I'll help out. More than that, you shouldn't be living alone."

"I like living alone." She wished he would hurry up and get to the point. Belle had never been claustrophobic, but she'd never been jammed into a storage closet with Darryl before, either. The man was practically inside of her. It wouldn't take more than a few quick moves...

What *was* she thinking of?

"I should move in with you," he said. "In case you suffer a fall or something."

She had felt a few twinges of worry these past weeks, especially when she'd had such a bad attack of nausea she'd been barely able to climb out of bed. But living with Darryl was unthinkable. "You must be crazy. We might as well take an ad in the newspaper and announce that you're the father. Would you like that?"

"No," he admitted. "But we could get around it."

"How?"

"We'll tell everybody I'm researching an article." He gave her a self-satisfied smile. "About how ignorant men are regarding pregnancy. I do plan to write it, Belle. It would be a real eye-opener for my readers.''

''You can open their eyes in somebody else's condo.'' This was the worst idea she had heard in a long time. ''I'll bet there are lots of pregnant single women who'd be thrilled to have you as their houseguest. But not me.''

''You need someone to wait on you,'' he continued in a soothing voice. ''To fetch pickles and ice cream in the middle of the night. To bring you crackers in bed. I could even drop you at work so you wouldn't have to drive.''

She wished the offer weren't so tempting. ''There's no way I'm going to let you use my name in your magazine.''

''I won't,'' he promised hastily. ''I'll give you a pseudonym.''

''As if everybody wouldn't know—''

''I'll interview other women and create a composite,'' Darryl improvised. Why was he so determined to get her to agree to this?

She doubted he had been overwhelmed by paternal feelings when he'd seen the ultrasound. Her own reaction had been strong and deep. The instant she had seen the baby Belle had discovered that she would go to any lengths to protect it.

She would almost be willing to let Darryl hang around in case of emergency. Almost, but not quite. Besides, there wasn't going to be an emergency.

''I'll think about it,'' she said.

''Think about it now.''

''I've got work to do,'' she retorted. ''I'm hungry, my feet hurt, my stomach feels like an oil slick...''

''It does, huh?'' Without waiting for an invitation, he pulled up Belle's blouse and ran his hand across her tummy. ''That doesn't feel oily, it feels soft.''

''Only because your hand is covered with calluses,'' she protested.

"That's from playing volleyball." He didn't take his hand away, though. In fact, Darryl seemed to be enjoying probing underneath her blouse.

"What are you doing?" Belle demanded.

"Seeing if I can feel the baby."

"It's too small. Even I can't feel it yet," she said. "Besides, the baby isn't up *there*."

His hands had found the sports bra she'd worn, due to the fact that she had outgrown her regular ones. Through the soft fabric, his fingers probed her nipples. "Pregnancy really does make you larger, doesn't it?"

She tried to pull back, but there was no room to retreat. She grabbed Darryl's wrists, only to find he was too strong to push away. Besides, his persistent kneading was sending heat waves through her body. It made a nice change from nausea.

"They say women get very sensual during pregnancy," he murmured, sliding his hands beneath the elastic waistband and down her hips. His body pressed into hers, taut and hungry and hard. Definitely hard.

She wanted to object. Maybe in a few minutes . . .

Darryl curved over her, his mouth descending toward hers. Then he stopped.

"What?" said Belle.

"Are you going to bite me?"

"I might."

With a groan, he moved away. At least, he lifted his hands and retreated an inch or two, which was the most the storeroom would allow. His breathing was abnormally loud, and she was grateful that the sound masked her own sharp breaths.

"I guess we can forget that idea," she said. "If you move in, there'll be nothing but trouble."

Darryl blinked as if emerging from a daze. "Don't be ridiculous. Think of the massages I could give you. And my article—Belle, you'd be educating not only me but men all over the country to be more sympathetic to women."

"You really intend to write an educational article?" she asked.

He nodded.

"And not mention my name?"

He gave another, somewhat less vigorous nod.

Belle shook her head. "Nope. You couldn't hack it."

That brought his head up in defiance. "Excuse me?"

"Are you telling me you really want to know what pregnancy's like?" she demanded. "Every minute of it? Well, you can't. You might take time off work to go to the doctor's appointments and you might even try swallowing those humongous vitamin pills. But you won't wake up five times a night to go to the bathroom. And you certainly can't experience labor."

"I can cater to your every whim," he offered.

Now, there was a fabulous idea. Her every whim. Well, not *every* whim. Belle had no intention of landing in bed with the man again.

Maybe that was what he had in mind. She couldn't imagine why Darryl would be lusting after her, but it appeared to be the case. If so, he was in for a major disappointment.

He deserved it.

"You'll rub my back?" she pressed.

"I will."

"Whenever I like?"

"Within reason."

That seemed fair enough. Besides, what if she *did* have some serious problem in the middle of the night? "We can give it a try," she said. "Now will you let me out of the closet?"

"Certainly." Darryl opened the door with a flourish and bowed as she swept outside.

As soon as she'd taken a few breaths of fresh air, Belle realized she'd made a very risky decision. But what was life without a few risks?

Already, she couldn't wait until her first back rub.

6

ADJUSTING COPY to make it fit around ads was not Darryl's favorite task, and today he'd had to do it with two stories that he particularly liked.

He couldn't afford to cut the ads, so he had to trim the articles. One was the main piece on "New Sports and Old: How to Choose What's Right for You." The other was a wickedly funny item called "Which Babe Tonight? Coordinate Your Date with Your Activity."

Belle would dislike it when it came out in February. But not as much as she would dislike the article Darryl planned to publish in March.

Remembering the warm feel of her body beneath his in the closet a few days ago, he hoped she wouldn't hate it too much. Surely she could understand that men deserved a fair shake when it came to custody issues.

Besides, emphasizing men's fitness for parenthood also highlighted their responsibilities. And as for his thesis that men were superior, Belle was enough of a journalist to recognize the shock value of overstatement.

Tapping his fingers on his mouse pad, Darryl contemplated the fact that he would be moving in with her tomorrow. He would have to make sure their relationship remained platonic. It was what they both wanted, after all.

He still couldn't figure out why he'd responded the way he had in the storage closet. Belle wasn't the easygoing type of woman toasted and celebrated in *About Town*. Moreover, her waistline was expanding rapidly.

That was the odd thing. Instead of finding her less attractive as she burgeoned, Darryl found himself more drawn to her.

She seemed to embody an essential life force that was, unexpectedly, proving more desirable to him than the glitzy sexuality displayed by centerfold models in skimpy swimsuits. But surely close proximity would soon dull the edge of her appeal.

Darryl opened a new file in his computer to rough out an opening for his story. He tried a couple of titles, but "The Natural Superiority of Fathers" was the one that stuck.

If he put it on the cover, it was eye-catching enough to insure expanded news-rack sales for the magazine. In order to justify such an outrageous title, though, he knew he needed an equally in-your-face opening to the story.

His fingers began to tap.

"Until the modern era, a woman played the leading role in only one theatrical-style production—her wedding," he wrote. "Today's female, however, has created a new showcase for herself. It's called pregnancy."

What an opening paragraph! Darryl thought as he resumed his attack on the keys. Who could resist reading further?

"What was once a private matter has been dragged onto center stage. Today's woman and her expanding belly are applauded by an audience of ultrasound technicians, obstetricians, childbirth coaches and specialty shopkeepers. The man is relegated to a supporting role, if any.

"It's time someone told the truth. Gestating and delivering a baby are innate biological functions for which the mother deserves no more credit than the father. It's something that happens to her, not something on which she should pride herself."

He let out a low whistle. A lot of women would be furious. But if they read further, they would discover that he had some valid points.

"Our assumption that women are more fit to raise their offspring has led to an unfair system in which men are often denied the right to be parents. The result is uninvolved fathers, heartbroken children and, all too often, impoverished mothers."

With the names and details changed, he described how Jim had lost custody of his son. He emphasized the close bond between the two, and the unfairness of the wife's decision to move away.

Darryl pointed out that Jim had given up smoking during his wife's pregnancy, but that she had not. Still, that wasn't exactly evidence of superiority. He would need to dig up some better examples.

Putting the article aside, he went back to editing other people's writing. He would keep his eyes open for further anecdotes that would bear out the theme.

A while later, Jim himself arrived with photographic proofs for an upcoming issue. Darryl showed his friend what he'd written and received an appreciative clap on the back in response.

"If you want more examples, you should come to my noncustodial fathers' support group," said the photographer. "I've heard tales that made my beard curl."

"I'll take all the help I can get." They made a date for the following week.

Then Greg came in to discuss changing the format for movie reviews. Before Darryl knew it, the day and part of the evening had flown.

It was Friday night, and tomorrow he was scheduled to move into Belle's condo. He planned to spend the evening attending a mad round of parties before temporarily giving up his freedom.

"WHAT CLOWN NAMED this 'morning sickness'?" Belle demanded as she struggled to subdue her stomach while writing a caption on a photo of an obnoxiously slender model. "It's past dinnertime, and I've still got it."

Anita Rios handed her a bran muffin. "Try this. I'm featuring the recipe this month. It's got grated apples and zucchini in it. And honey for sweetening. Well, not just honey. Brown sugar, too."

"It's delicious."

"And good for you."

"Well, let's not exaggerate." Belle had written the headline on Anita's column herself: "Muffin Madness. High Fiber, Low Fat, Huge Taste!" Only farther down in the article would readers discover that low fat didn't mean low calorie.

She declined a second muffin. Even writing headlines on food articles seemed to make Belle gain weight. Self-consciously, she stroked one hand across her stomach.

"Oh, goodness, aren't you over that pregnancy thing yet?" Sandra swung into the office in a cloud of silk and expensive perfume. Orchids wove around her hat and trailed down her back, matching the flowers painted on her white two-piece dress.

"Gestation still takes nine months," Belle informed the publisher.

"Oh, does it?" Sandra's blue eyes widened. "I know so little about children—I keep mistaking them for mice. When one enters the room, I scream. You aren't planning on bringing it to work, are you?"

"I'll find day-care," Belle assured her, although that was a prospect she wasn't ready to consider. The emergence of an actual baby remained in the realm of the theoretical.

"Have we heard from that mall lady about an appointment?" Sandra asked.

"Not yet. I thought she was going to call you at home."

"Oh, was she?" One hand fluttered in the air. "I suppose she did say that."

Belle wished her former roommate would pay more attention to the details of business. If not for the lawyer who oversaw her investments, Sandra would probably have forgotten where she kept all those millions of dollars.

At least she *had* promised to organize their formal presentation for cosponsoring the mall's opening, once they got the go-ahead from Mira. That was a relief. Belle had enough work to do without adding a major project like that.

Anita checked her watch. "Maybe we should hit the road."

The publisher smiled. "Oh, yes, let's! Wait till you see the spread at the Hendersons'! They're using Chef François and he makes an incredible pâté!"

Anita was researching an article to be called "Cater Your Own Wedding: Banquets on a Budget." Sandra had offered to take the food editor to some of her friends' parties that night to steal ideas.

Belle waved goodbye, then sat staring at the photo of the skinny model and wondered if the woman ever went on eating binges. Or got pregnant. Or lost her mind and agreed to let some Neanderthal specimen like Darryl Horak move into her apartment.

Belle didn't even like female roommates. What on earth was she going to do with the editor of *About Town*?

He would criticize her mismatched furniture, take over the remote control and probably fill the condo with the nasal whine of football announcers. She wondered if it was possible to tune the TV permanently to PBS.

There was still time to change her mind, she supposed. True, she had given Darryl a duplicate house key, but she could simply demand its return.

The more she thought about it, the more Belle felt she would be doing them both a favor. Allowing Darryl to move in was tempting fate.

They might kill each other. They might even succumb to that bizarre recurring attraction that must be an after-effect of the aphrodisiac in the punch.

A few back rubs and a promise to fetch pickles and ice cream at midnight weren't worth days of inconvenience and discomfort. Why hadn't she given more thought to what it would mean, having a man on the premises?

No more wandering around in her underwear. No more lolling on the couch like a beached whale, groaning aloud until Placido Domingo soothed her alpha waves. No more evening-long marathons watching tapes of ice skating from Olympics past.

She should call him now. The clock was edging toward eight, later than she'd realized.

After checking the phone book, she dialed the *About Town* offices, but reached only voice-mail. She tried to find a home number for Darryl, but it wasn't listed.

Well, she would simply have to send him packing when he arrived tomorrow. That would be soon enough, Belle decided as she collected her purse and headed for the door. At least she needn't confront the man tonight, with her feet sore and her abdominal muscles aching.

SITTING IN HIS CAR, Darryl stared at the beach half a block from his house. It was a sorry world when a self-confident single man with a credit card and wheels could neither find a party nor start one of his own.

The November moon shone bleakly over an almost deserted strand. It was too late in the season for barbecues, and the only lovers strolling here tonight were more interested in getting their dogs to poop below the waterline than in exchanging romantic caresses.

He checked his watch. Twenty-three-forty hours. Not even midnight.

With a grunt, Darryl removed his car keys and strode along the oceanfront sidewalk. He didn't intend to go home, but that's where his legs were carrying him.

His neighbors, he noticed, had finally removed the pumpkin and witch decorations from their windows and replaced them with turkeys and Pilgrims. Judging by the rough edges on the paper cutouts, their children had made the things in preschool.

Frowning, he wondered whether his baby would ever go to preschool, and realized that of course it would. He had to stop picturing a baby perpetually babbling in its crib. How fast did they grow, anyway? At what point did they start blaming their parents for the world's problems?

His house was tiny, a one-story white adobe wedged between duplexes. Prices at the beach were astronomical, and he'd been lucky to be able to afford this one. It wouldn't accommodate much more than a solitary bachelor, though, Darryl reflected as he entered.

The living room was barely big enough to swing a cat. The kitchen begged for the suffix "ette" on the end, and if the health service ever checked behind the refrigerator, Darryl was due for a long stretch in the slammer.

He flicked on the light in the bedroom and tried to visualize it through Belle's eyes. He noted the out-of-date wood paneling, the curtains dotted with ducks and the latest Flaunt It centerfold hanging on the wall. No wonder she'd bitten him.

A surge of energy told Darryl he couldn't bear to spend the night lounging around in front of the TV. He might as well pack and move into Belle's place right now.

She couldn't be asleep yet. Even two-year-olds stayed up later than this in Los Angeles.

Besides, he'd promised to wait on her, hadn't he? He might as well start with breakfast tomorrow.

Invigorated by his decision, Darryl pulled a suitcase from the closet and threw in some clothes, his shaving kit, shampoo and hair dryer. He nearly added a packet of condoms, then realized he was three months too late.

Staring at the suitcase, he noticed that he'd forgotten underwear, and tossed in a few days' worth. He decided to take the perishables from the fridge, too, until a cursory inspection revealed that they had already perished.

He locked the house behind him, hopped into his car and set off for Palms. He knew the way, sort of. It wasn't far, as Los Angeles geography went.

The problem was that the authorities had installed a new freeway that hijacked his lane when Darryl wasn't expecting it. Before he could figure it out, he found himself making an unscheduled landing at Los Angeles International Airport. It took half an hour just to find his way back.

He refused to ask directions. Only tourists did that.

It was nearly 1:00 a.m. by the time he located Palms, and he was beginning to doubt that Belle would still be awake. That was the advantage of having a key. He could quietly establish himself in the spare bedroom and surprise her with breakfast.

The condo complex turned out to be five units along a driveway that ran at right angles to the street. The lot was narrow and deep, the structures solid but not showy.

After parking, he proceeded along the walkway to unit C. Holding the suitcase to his left hand, Darryl fished the key from his pocket and inserted it into the door. A copy of a copy, the key grated reluctantly into place but refused to turn.

He jiggled the thing, but it still wouldn't move. Baring his teeth, he twisted as hard as he could and threw his weight against the door.

Everything gave way at once. The key turned, the door flew open and Darryl plunged into the living room, fell over his suitcase and crashed to the floor.

Rubbing his hip, he waited tensely for Belle to come storming out, but she didn't. He recalled hearing that pregnant women slept very soundly.

He was about to get up when he heard a click, like someone cocking a gun. The odd part was that it came from the outer doorway, not from the direction of the bedrooms.

Great. Darryl had arrived at Belle's condo only to provide free admittance to a mugger. This was not going to look good either in the article or in his obituary, whichever came first.

"Put your hands up, you lowlife creep." Despite its dryness, the voice bristled with authority. "Way up!" The shadowy figure in the doorway didn't sound like a mugger. It didn't look like one, either. Too thin, too short and too dressed in a nightgown.

Darryl put his hands up. "I know how this looks, but Belle gave me a key," he said.

"Belle would never give a man her key," said the woman.

"I'm Darryl Horak." When that name didn't evoke instant recognition, he added, "I'm staying with her to research a story on pregnant women."

To his vast relief, Darryl saw moonlight glint off the gun barrel as it was lowered. "Oh, you're that man on the beach! The one who took our pictures."

The woman reached for the light switch, and a blinding brilliance smashed into his face. Both of them stood blinking for a while, and then he recognized the octogenarian who had worn a bikini along with Belle's other recruits in the centerfold picture on the beach.

"I'm Belle's neighbor, Moira McGregor." She stuck out her hand, then noticed the gun and transferred it to her left before extending the right again.

Darryl shook it. "Sorry about the noise. I'm supposed to move in tomorrow but I couldn't sleep."

"Belle can, obviously." The woman squinted at him as if double-checking his identity. "Well, I guess she knows what she's doing. Say, you folks need any more models, you just let me know. I'm not as shy as I used to be about my body. There's a lot of old geezers who buy magazines like yours and they get tired of those young girlies."

"That's why we took your picture," Darryl said by way of sidestepping the issue. "Maybe you'd better get back to sleep now." Realizing she might resent the implication, he added, "Not that you need it. But you probably left some young stud in your bed and he might get lonely."

Moira chuckled. "In my dreams. But thank you." And out she went.

Darryl shut the door behind her, then rubbed his sore hip and examined the room. What a load of mismatched junk. Where did Belle get her furniture, the city dump?

A deep yawn reminded him that even masculine vigor doesn't last forever. One bedroom had the door tightly shut, so he hauled his suitcase into the other one.

Switching on the light, he discovered that it contained a daybed too short for his six-foot-one-inch frame. The sheets smelled dusty, and the pillow was flat as a doormat. Other than that, the room contained only a bedside table and a desk so fragile it looked as if a heavy wind might carry it off.

With the sense of having arrived in a strange hotel in a city where no one spoke English, he popped open his suitcase and began to unpack.

BELLE LAY IN BED trying to levitate a box of crackers from the kitchen to her bedroom, but it didn't work. Then she remembered that she had been dreaming about Darryl Horak.

In the dream, he had moved in with a camera crew, two models in bathing suits and his art director. Every time Belle had shuffled into the kitchen or needed to use the bathroom, they'd all followed her.

The truth probably wouldn't be much different. This was Darryl's day to show up on her doorstep, and she doubted she would know peace again until she got rid of him.

Belle wondered what time he would arrive and hoped it would be sometime next year. Or the year after. Or maybe in time for his child's high school graduation.

Clenching her teeth, she rolled out of bed. After washing up, she pulled on her bathrobe and started down the hall.

A noise from the spare bedroom sent her heart skittering into her throat. Spiders and crickets made periodic invasions of the premises, but she had never had to contend with anything loud enough to snuffle. The sound came again, and resolved itself into breathing.

A large animal. The only animal that big would be a bear or a human, or possibly Darryl Horak.

Nudging open the door, Belle spotted the subject of her nightmare. She couldn't believe the man had had the nerve to move in while she slept. It was an affront to decency, even if they had once been intimate.

Pushing the door wider, she anchored herself with a hand on the frame and studied her unwelcome guest. He sprawled across the daybed, his feet sticking over the end. When she'd bought the thing, it hadn't seemed particularly small, but then, she hadn't bought it with a six-foot-something male in mind.

From here, she had a pretty good view of his body, covered only by a pair of tiny black underpants. Lord, the man *was* built like an Adonis. It was too bad to waste a body like that on such an annoying personality.

As if on command, he groaned and rolled over, crushing his dark hair against the pillow. Now she got a clear look at Darryl's features. In sleep, his mouth seemed softer and his cheeks had a gently rounded sweetness, almost like a child's.

Belle was dismayed by the illusion of innocence. Seeing him this way, she could even imagine that he had once been a child. The horrifying conclusion was that this tiny creature inside her might someday grow up to be just like Daddy.

It had to be a girl, she decided. Then she would never gaze into her child's eyes and see Darryl staring back at her.

And he *was* staring. The man had come fully awake without passing through that dazed state that, for her, usually lasted half an hour.

Too late, Belle realized that she had left her bathrobe gaping open, revealing a short nightie that clung to her curves. Her guest's eyes opened, and opened some more, and then got wider still.

She hoped he was enjoying the view. It was, she felt determined, the last time he would ever see it.

7

"NO," DARRYL SAID for the third time. "I am not leaving."

They sat at the kitchen table, each wrapped in a robe. He was consuming coffee and a nonfat coffee cake that he'd taken from Belle's freezer without asking permission.

She was drinking tea with her toast and trying not to gag at the smell of coffee. "You can't live here," she said. "You don't even fit in the bed." Surely he would acknowledge that point, at least.

"We could share yours," Darryl suggested between mouthfuls.

"We tried that, and look where it got us."

"Come on! Our situation isn't that bad." He leaned back, his long legs intruding into Belle's space until she kicked him in the ankle. Then he swung them lazily away.

"Oh, it isn't?"

"Look at it this way." Darryl's eyes glittered. "We both like being single, right? But sooner or later we were likely to get the urge to have children, especially you."

"Me?"

"The way I see it, you're the big winner in all this," her unwanted tenant continued, ignoring her sarcastic tone. "Women get this big maternal urge in their thirties. Well, I've taken care of that for you."

"How kind," Belle growled.

"I don't see why you're being such a bad sport." He took another swig of coffee. "You don't see me complaining."

"What do you have to complain about?" she demanded. "Other than the fact that I may garnishee half your paycheck for the rest of your life."

That stopped him. It was at least thirty seconds before Darryl resumed tearing apart the coffee cake. Then he said, "We'll reach a financial arrangement, I'm sure. But you've already got a two-bedroom condo. How much more could it cost to raise a kid?"

"I'll have my lawyer draw up an accounting," she said. "Now would you please go home?"

"In a month or so. We've got the issue all planned, with my article on the cover. Can't let down the troops, can we?" He got up and went to pour himself a second cup of coffee.

She didn't understand why he was being so stubborn. The man couldn't enjoy her company. These days, Belle didn't even enjoy her own company. And surely he could research that article without physically imposing on a pregnant female.

Besides, it was only two weeks until Thanksgiving, and she had plans. She hadn't confirmed them, but they had taken on the solidity of accomplished fact in her mind.

"My parents are coming for Thanksgiving," she said. "They'll be staying with me, so I'll need the bedroom."

She didn't intend to admit that her folks always preferred to stay in their enormous motor home. For two years, since her father's retirement, they'd been crisscrossing the country. Belle wanted them to be able to stay with her, if they chose to.

"They don't live in the area?" Darryl said.

"No." She explained about their long-suppressed love of travel. "They don't have a permanent address. When they go overseas, they leave the camper at my sister's house in Maryland. It's just a short connecting flight to Miami or New York.''

"Sounds like a nice life." He appeared lost in reflection, no doubt trying to figure out how to maneuver her into letting him stay.

"As a matter of fact, they're going on a Caribbean cruise for Christmas and New Year's," Belle went on. "Which makes it especially important that I see them at Thanksgiving."

"That's quite a drive," he said. "I mean, if they plan to leave here at the end of November and drop their motor home in Maryland by the middle of December."

"They're used to driving." He did have a point, though. Belle's parents hadn't promised they would come to California.

When had she invited them? Last August or September, she recalled. And, with a jolt, she realized she hadn't talked to them in more than a month.

"Have you told them yet?" Darryl asked. "About the baby?"

She shook her head. The last time she'd spoken to them, they'd been visiting friends in Las Vegas. There'd been loud voices in the background, and she hadn't felt comfortable bringing up such a sensitive topic.

Besides, she'd intended to convey the news in person, at Thanksgiving. That way she could explain the circumstances in detail.

But it surprised her that she hadn't heard from them in four weeks. They must have gotten caught up in seeing shows and playing the slot machines. Between morning sickness and work, she'd lost track of the time and hadn't thought to call them, either.

"We're not as close as we used to be," Belle admitted. "I was sort of their favorite, growing up. I was the one who starred in the class play and won a scholarship. They were always telling me how proud they were."

"Brothers and sisters?" he asked.

"A younger sister," she said. "Bari and I competed a lot." She felt sad, realizing that their instinctive rivalry had kept the two of them from becoming close. It hadn't helped that Belle had almost always come out ahead in the academic realm.

"What does she do in Maryland?" Darryl returned the remaining coffee cake to the refrigerator and rinsed his plate and cup. Score one for him, Belle thought.

"She's a homemaker with a four-year-old daughter." Belle was getting an uncomfortable feeling. If her parents were going to be island-hopping over Christmas, wouldn't they want to spend Thanksgiving with their granddaughter?

But they *had* to come here. Something about pregnancy made her feel young and vulnerable. She wanted her mother to fuss over her and her father to shake his head in that indulgent, look-what-Belle's-up-to-now way of his.

"I'll bet they just dote on that kid," Darryl observed as he washed his hands.

"Mikki's a cute little girl," she admitted.

Very cute. And in the four years since the first grandchild had been born, Belle had ceased to be the center of her parents' attention. Until this moment she hadn't realized it, but Bari had won their lifelong competition by the world's oldest stealth tactic: having a child.

Now it's my turn. But this wasn't a competition. Becoming a mother made her feel closer to her sister. She wished Bari didn't live so far away.

"Maybe they're not coming for Thanksgiving." Darryl turned at the sink, one eyebrow arching. "Maybe I can stay here, after all."

"They're coming!" she insisted. "And you're going!"

"Why don't you give them a call? If they can't make it, you might be glad to have me around. I've always wanted to try cooking a turkey."

"Good idea—the phone call, not the turkey. I'd like to confirm when they're arriving." Trying to act unworried, Belle marched into the bedroom and dialed the number of her parents' cellular phone. It rang three times before someone picked it up.

"Yes?" Her mother always sounded hesitant when answering, as if afraid there might be a salesman or an extraterrestrial at the other end.

"Mom, it's Belle." Her spirits rose as she heard her mother call the news to her father, then deflated as he growled back, "Where's she been, anyway? Too busy to talk to her parents?"

"Belle?" said her mother into the phone. "We've been trying to reach you for weeks."

"You have?" she frowned. "I haven't received any messages."

Come to think of it, she hadn't been getting messages from anybody except at the office. With a sinking sensation, Belle glanced at the bedside machine.

The tiny red "On" panel was dark. She must have accidentally turned the thing off.

"Well, we've called several times," said her mother. "I know we talked about coming out for Thanksgiving, but we just can't disappoint Mikki. We promised we'd be at her house. You're welcome to join us."

Belle was tempted, but in her present state of discomfort, she couldn't face crowded airports, delayed flights and narrow airline seats. Besides, flying wasn't recommended for pregnant women, was it?

"I can't," she said. "But, Mom, I need to see you guys. Couldn't you swing by here before you head east?"

"Honey, we're in Kentucky. We can hardly 'swing by' California." That was one of the maddening things about cellular phones. Until this moment, Belle had assumed her parents were still in Nevada. "If you can't make it to Maryland, we'll try to visit you next spring."

Belle was on the point of arguing, but stopped. She didn't want little Mikki to be disappointed at Thanksgiving, did she? And her parents had a right to enjoy their granddaughter.

It flashed into her mind that she ought to tell her mother about the pregnancy right now. Frantically, Belle searched for the right words. She couldn't just blurt it out. A matter like this required a certain delicacy.

Then her father called out that he needed to phone the highway patrol to report a wreck they were passing on the interstate. "Two cars and a horse trailer. They'll need help pronto!"

"I've got to go," her mother said. "Is everything okay with you?"

"Fine," said Belle. "You'd better call the cops in case somebody's hurt."

As she hung up, a weight settled onto her shoulders. She'd never been sentimental about holidays. And she'd believed she had long ago weaned herself from relying on her parents emotionally.

Yet at this moment she felt abandoned. Maybe it was due to hormones, but Belle had never experienced such a wave of loneliness.

Her emotionalism distressed her even further. How could she pity herself when in Kentucky two cars and a horse trailer had just collided? Why was she blowing this situation out of proportion?

Rational arguments didn't help. Darn it, she *was* alone, and she felt like a little kid.

To Belle's dismay, tears overflowed, spattering the pinks and purples on her quilt.

STANDING IN THE HALL outside the bedroom, Darryl couldn't believe it. He'd overheard enough to realize Belle's parents weren't going to make it for Thanksgiving, but he was surprised to see how deeply it affected her.

Since his own father had died and his mother had moved too far away for frequent visits, Darryl had filled the holidays with charity and promotional events, plus throwing parties for his pals. But he supposed that expecting a baby might make a woman want to have family around.

Well, he was living here, so it was up to him to do something, he decided.

Belle didn't seem to notice when he entered the room. She was too busy snuffling into a wad of tissues, her shoulders shaking with grief.

Darryl couldn't help feeling sorry for her. A woman had a right to miss her mother at a time like this. Besides, she looked cute curled around a Kleenex, her red mane wilting.

He sat on the edge of the bed. "I've got an idea."

"Uh-oh." Even sorrow couldn't quench Belle's sarcasm. "Why do I assume this has something to do with your staying?"

"We have to get this baby off to the right start," he said. "I propose we cook a turkey and invite our friends." When she didn't respond, he added, "Like I said, I'll cook the bird. You can take care of the side dishes." There was still no answer, so he continued, "Maybe some wild rice, or how about tabouli? A big salad and steamed broccoli. We could get some fat-free packaged stuffing, too."

"That's the most disgusting idea I ever heard." Belle emerged from behind her tissue, red-eyed but geared for battle. "Tabouli at Thanksgiving? Steamed broccoli? And you are not bringing any fat-free stuffing into my house, mister."

"Don't you want to eat healthy for the baby?" he asked.

"Not on Thanksgiving!" she said. "What were you planning to have for dessert, baked apples?"

"That sounds good." Darryl decided not to mention that he would prefer those apples baked in a shell and doused with butter, cinnamon and sugar. Everyone was entitled to a few weaknesses.

"You're un-American!" She snatched another wad of tissues and blew her nose loudly enough to throw a squadron of geese off-course. "Sweet potatoes buried beneath brown sugar and marshmallows! Stuffing loaded with turkey fat! Gravy and mashed potatoes, and if there's any broccoli to be found, it's drowning in cheese sauce. Got that?"

He shuddered. "Haven't you ever heard of cholesterol?"

"In my opinion, it's overrated," snapped Belle, and climbed off the bed, her tears forgotten.

His urge to argue died suddenly. At least she'd agreed to his suggestion. "The point is, we should celebrate Thanksgiving as a family."

"You're not my family," she said.

"I'm part of your baby's family," he countered. "And I always will be."

That remark stopped her in midstride. She sucked in a couple of long breaths.

Darryl, too, recognized that he'd hit on a basic truth. He really was going to be linked to Belle for the rest of their lives. Even if they married other people and lived far apart, they would always be this child's parents.

Someday that might be him sitting alone in a bedroom, talking on the telephone about a Thanksgiving celebration of which he wouldn't be a part. He tried not to dwell on the possibility that he had glimpsed the ghost of Thanksgiving future. The present was all he could handle right now.

"Sweet potatoes would be all right," he said. "And you could serve the broccoli with the cheese sauce on the side. Let's really have fun with this. Let's invite everyone we know."

"Greg and Janie would kill each other," she protested.

"They can put aside their petty squabbles for one day," Darryl said. "And so can we."

Belle's chin tilted upward as if she were about to dispute that possibility, but she must have seen the sincerity on his face.

"All right, I guess we can fix Thanksgiving dinner together." Suddenly she grinned, and he could have sworn her red hair perked up. "If nothing else, it'll shock the hell out of everybody."

BELLE GROANED INWARDLY when she returned from some last-minute grocery shopping and watched Darryl pry open the oven and baste the bird. Darryl, who wore jeans and a turtleneck beneath a spotless white apron and chef's hat, had managed to clean himself up but hadn't bothered with the kitchen.

It was on the tip of her tongue to point out that the kitchen was a mess, it was two o'clock, the guests were due to arrive at four and she had four items to make. Still, he *had* prepared the turkey, and stuffing to serve on the side, claiming it had less fat that way.

And the bird smelled terrific. Belle's morning sickness had finally subsided, and she could appreciate delicious scents again.

She had to admit, the past two weeks hadn't gone as badly as she'd feared. Darryl had made one attempt to reorganize her CD collection, but he'd given up under pressure. Otherwise, their contact had been limited to blearily sharing the breakfast table, ordering take-out food after returning home late from work and politely taking turns at the remote control.

The hardest part had been dealing with her friends' reactions. Issuing invitations for Thanksgiving had given Belle a chance to tell them about the living arrangement before they discovered it for themselves.

The response had been primarily disbelief. Eventually, though, everyone claimed to have accepted the explanation that Darryl was researching an article. And they'd almost all promised to come for the holiday dinner.

"Good, you're back," he called as he slid shut the oven door. "I'll get out of your way and let you cook."

Belle stayed where she was, deliberately blocking the exit. "Aren't you forgetting something?"

"What?" He gazed around innocently. "I don't think so."

Slowly and as obviously as possible, she eyed the grease drippings on the floor, the spatters and plastic wrap in which the turkey'd been encased on the counter and the cookbook sprawled on the table. "Try again."

Recognition dawned, followed by a shrug. "What's the point of cleaning up now? I figured we'd do it when you're finished cooking."

"Before or after I slip in the grease and suffer a miscarriage?" she asked.

He studied the area around his feet. "Gee, I didn't notice that. Do you have a mop or something?"

"Try the closet. I'll come back when you're done," she said.

Half an hour later, she was able to start cooking. Everything sounded easy: instant mashed potatoes, sweet-potato casserole, gravy from a mix, frozen green beans and almonds. But ingredients had to be mixed and measured, and nothing could be cooked too far in advance or it would all get cold.

The heat in the kitchen made her hair frizz, and after half an hour she felt like a refugee from a chain gang. When Darryl appeared in the doorway and asked those endearing words, "Can I help?" Belle actually felt a wave of liking for the man.

"I'm afraid I've made another mess." She pointed to some brown sugar spilled on the floor.

"Hey, today is supposed to be fun." He came forward and caught her shoulders. "I thought we were making Thanksgiving dinner together. You look like you're ready to burst into tears."

"I hate feeling like this," she admitted. "I get overwhelmed so easily."

"Will you kick me in a sensitive area if I point out that it's probably got something to do with impending motherhood?" he asked.

"That depends," she said. "What do you consider a sensitive area?"

"I'll tell you what." Darryl regarded the counter covered with boxes, pots, baking dishes and food. "Why don't you read that cookbook aloud, and I'll follow your directions?"

"Can I sit down?" she asked.

He pulled out a chair and dusted it off. "You are *required* to sit down."

Once she had her feet propped up, Belle's exhaustion waned. She was surprised to find she enjoyed instructing Darryl as he went about fixing the sweet-potato casserole. In a short time, the preparations were complete, leaving only the last-minute heating.

"I'm going to change," she said, slowly standing. "You can take a break. Watch football, if you want to. Or channel switch." It was the most generous offer she could think of, since even the distant sound of channel surfing gave her a headache.

"In a minute," he said. "I think I'll set the table first."

"Table?" Belle headed for the doorway. "Do you see a dining room? We're eating buffet style."

Darryl glided ahead of her, draped one arm across the door frame and leaned against it, his body looming over hers. "Oh, come on, we can improvise something. My mother would never have let us put her best china on our laps."

"China?" She couldn't believe the man's naiveté. "A long time ago, shortly after the Middle Ages, mankind devised a great and wondrous invention. It's called the paper plate."

"For Thanksgiving?" Shock registered on his face.

"They have little turkeys printed on them," Belle assured him. "Can I go now?"

"Not quite." He bent down, gave her a crooked smile and kissed her.

She tried to protest, but what came out was an undignified mumble. Apparently afraid that she would scold if she ever got free, Darryl kissed her again.

"You taste like spun sugar," he murmured.

"I had a few of the marshmallows," she admitted. She had no intention of letting on how much she enjoyed the hard, probing feel of his mouth. She would have served her guests frozen turkey dinners before she would have admitted that the pressure of his chest against hers was sending fingers of desire stroking her most private recesses. "Are you finished?"

"Not quite." Grasping her waist, Darryl arched over her and deepened the kiss, his tongue tracing the edges of her teeth while his hands explored upward.

The passion she'd been so studiously repressing raged through Belle like a forest fire. Forget Thanksgiving. Forget their friends. Hungrily, she seized his hips and began issuing a demand of her own.

That was when her phone rang. At the same time, Darryl's flip phone began to buzz. And both their pagers went off.

They drew apart reluctantly, their eyes meeting in mutual dismay. "I have a bad feeling about this," said Belle.

"How bad can it be?" said Darryl.

"I guess we're about to find out," she said.

8

THINGS WENT FROM BAD to worse as they answered and returned their calls.

Belle's neighbor, Moira, had encountered car trouble and was stuck at a friend's house twenty miles away, where she had no choice but to stay for dinner.

Anita Rios had contracted food poisoning from a new dish she'd whipped up that morning. She would be spending the day in bed.

Elva was "on a roll" in her studio and couldn't tear herself away from creating the world's next masterpiece.

Janie had decided it was courting disaster to attend the same meal as Greg, and bowed out. Greg had decided the same thing.

Unfortunately, Darryl and Belle didn't discover that neither of the pair was coming until they were both off the phone. Darryl didn't have Greg's home number with him, and at Janie's house a machine answered.

"Who does that leave?" Belle asked as they stood alone in the living room. "Anybody?"

"Just Mindy," Darryl said.

Belle couldn't place the name. "Who's Mindy?"

"Miss March," he said, folding away his flip phone.

"You invited your girlfriend?" she asked. "I can't believe it."

His jaw tightened. "She's not my girlfriend. She keeps hanging around the office and she mentioned she didn't have anywhere to go for Thanksgiving."

Only a man would take such a hint at face value. "She was wangling for an invitation all right, but not to *my* house! She wanted to spend the holiday with you."

He started to laugh. "I guess you're right. Gee, this should be some party."

"I don't believe it." Belle sank onto the couch. "Just the three of us for Thanksgiving dinner. You, me and a skinny model who's got the hots for you. What fun!"

The doorbell rang.

"The turkey should be nearly done." Darryl fled toward the kitchen. "I'll check."

"Coward!" she yelled.

The woman who stood on the tiny porch sported a mass of dark hair and a formfitting pink pantsuit. "Hi!" she said, handing over the biggest potted chrysanthemum Belle had ever seen. "You must be Darryl's sister."

"He doesn't have a sister." She knew she shouldn't yield to temptation, but she couldn't help adding, "I'm just the mother of his child."

Mindy's eyes grew to the size of compact discs and her bright pink lips began to tremble. Then she smiled. "Oh! What a joker! You're Belle Martens, aren't you? You edit that wonderful magazine! But...is this *your* condo?"

The awe in her voice softened Belle's resentment. It wasn't Mindy's fault that Darryl had invited her. "Yes. We're having dinner for our friends. Smoking the peace pipe, so to speak."

The model made no motion to enter. "I don't smoke."

"Neither do we, not literally," Belle said.

"Who else is coming?" The woman regarded her dubiously. It struck Belle that Mindy, like everyone else, must know about the night she and Darryl might or might not have spent together. The last thing an ambitious model wanted was to risk antagonizing either of them.

She felt a wave of sympathy. "Actually, nobody. It's been a comedy of errors. But—"

"I only dropped by to say I couldn't come, either." Mindy began edging away. "I'm so sorry."

"Your flowers!" Belle held them out.

"Please accept them as a thank-you gift. For inviting me!" The model scuttled backward in a series of nervous hops.

"We've got plenty of food," Belle said. "Really."

"My family came to town unexpectedly. But thank you both so much!" Mindy pivoted on her high heels and fled down the walkway.

Belle wished the woman weren't in such a hurry. They really did have a lot of food. And she hoped Mindy really did have another invitation so she wouldn't go hungry on Thanksgiving, until she remembered that models never ate, anyway.

"Was that her?" Darryl appeared from the kitchen, holding a meat thermometer.

"She couldn't stay," Belle said. "Actually, when she saw me, she ran out of here like the hounds of hell were after her."

They exchanged glances, and then they both started to laugh. "We'll be eating this food until Christmas," he said.

"That's okay. I like turkey leftovers."

Darryl grinned. "Me, too. And that reminds me of something we were doing before we were so rudely interrupted."

That was one advantage of being alone together, Belle thought. What could be better than a feast à deux, with a little cuddling thrown in for good measure? "Okay, but I'm starved. Is the turkey nearly done?"

He glanced at the thermometer in his hand. "I'm not sure. This thing is broken. It hasn't moved."

"That doesn't mean the thermometer's broken, Darryl."

"It doesn't?"

"It means the turkey isn't cooked."

He frowned. "Of course it's cooked. It's been roasting for six hours."

That sounded long enough, all right, but thermometers rarely lied. "You did defrost it, didn't you?"

"Of course." He flexed his shoulders. "I put it in the fridge yesterday morning."

Belle hated to spoil his cheerful mood, but sooner or later the truth would come out. "It takes three or four days to defrost a turkey in the refrigerator."

"That's ridiculous," he said. "Really?"

Something else occurred to her. "If the turkey was still frozen, how did you remove the giblets?"

"The what?" he said.

Belle wondered if there were any institutions that took terminally befuddled males, then realized that if there were, they would already be full. "We could go out to eat," she said.

"Out?" He still hadn't grasped the magnitude of his mistake. "Frozen or not, the thing's got to get done sometime."

"Midnight?" she hazarded. "In any case, by the time the center is cooked, the outside will be dry as leather."

"You're making this up," he said.

"Go stick your hand in the middle of the turkey," she suggested.

His lips pressed together, Darryl retreated into the kitchen. Banging noises indicated that he was removing the turkey from the oven and, presumably, checking the cavity.

"Gee, there's stuff in here," he called. "Why is it wrapped in paper?"

"Because those are the giblets and you're supposed to take them out before you cook the turkey." Belle strolled in and stood behind him. "People make gravy out of them."

"It's ice cold in the middle." He eyed the turkey as if it had committed a personal affront.

On the outside, the bird had turned an alluring brown and was issuing a mouth-watering aroma. "Let's hack off some pieces and broil them," Belle suggested.

"Can we do that?" he asked.

"I won't tell if you won't."

DARRYL WAS SURPRISED to find that Thanksgiving dinner tasted just as good on a paper plate as on a china one. Belle had been right about a lot of things tonight, he supposed.

It hurt to admit it, but he'd made some bonehead mistakes. He should have researched turkey cooking more thoroughly and not merely gotten verbal instructions from Elva.

Darryl was embarrassed to realize he'd assumed that fixing a turkey must be a simple matter because women did it all the time. Recognizing that he'd drawn a false conclusion didn't invalidate the theme of his article, though. He still felt men got a raw deal when it came to parenting, particularly in custody disputes.

Attending a fathers' meeting with Jim last week had provided more than enough anecdotes for his story. Some of the men had told horror stories about ex-wives who used the children to punish them for imagined wrongs. Most of them had sounded desperately lonely for their kids, and had made sacrifices in their lives to ensure continuing contact.

In a few cases, he suspected the men hadn't been telling the whole story, and he supposed that women in a similar group would have equally miserable tales to tell. But Darryl had noticed that TV shows and books usually told the women's side, while hardly anyone spoke up for the men.

He was no longer writing the article merely to make a point, nor to draw attention to his magazine. These guys had bared their souls, and Darryl owed them the fair hearing some of them hadn't received in divorce court.

He hoped Belle would understand that the article wasn't directed at her, even though he might weave in a few funny anecdotes about her pregnancy. Surely she could understand the need to mix humor with pathos.

Across the kitchen table, the object of his musings sat consuming her dinner with gusto. He admired her restraint in not continuing to twit him about the turkey.

The broiled chunks were delicious. And Belle had been right about the sweet-potato casserole. Empty calories or not, it was the star of the show.

A wave of well-being swept over Darryl. "This is great," he said.

Belle eyed him warily. "You didn't mind helping me with my half of the meal?"

"This is *our* meal," he said. Seeing her dubious expression, he added, "Everything's perfect. It may surprise you to know that, tonight, I have no criticisms of you whatsoever."

Apparently she wasn't about to take his declaration at face value. "What about the way I organize things? I heard you cussing earlier about trying to find a pan."

"Well, I think that 'organize things' would be using the term loosely. But it's better than the way you store your CDs," he said.

"What's wrong with them?" Her voice bristled with challenge.

"Oh, nothing." Darryl knew he should stop there, but he couldn't restrain a touch of sarcasm. "I *like* the way half of them are in the wrong cases. It makes picking music like a lottery. When I actually get the artist I want, I feel as if I've won a prize!"

After a moment's glare, Belle broke into a grin. "All right, I'll admit I can never find the CD I want, either. But if I keep shuffling them around, sooner or later they'll end up in the right boxes."

He was in no mood to argue the point. "What kind of pie did you get?"

"Apple, pumpkin and pecan."

"All three?"

"I was expecting eight people," she reminded him.

"Great," he said. "I'll have a piece of each."

So did Belle, adding a big scoop of vanilla ice cream for each of them. Here was a woman after his own heart.

As they ate, Darryl found himself watching her. He had never seen a woman with such velvety skin. Maybe it was the effect of pregnancy, but everything about her appeared vibrant. Her eyes smoldered and her cheeks curved with such round firmness that he ached to cup her face in his hands.

In the soft light, her hair glinted like copper. She resembled a woman from a Rembrandt painting, he thought, timeless and rich in life.

"I'll clean up," Darryl said as she finished.

"Thanks," she said. "I think I'll stretch out on the couch."

She sailed from the room, and he whisked the paper plates into the trash, then made foil packets of the leftovers and cleaned the pans. He even remembered to wash the floor, which had gotten dirty again.

In the back of his mind, Darryl had been contemplating a return to that passionate scene in the doorway, which had been so rudely interrupted by the phones. Now he discovered he was too stuffed to contemplate anything more than lazing around listening to music.

A quick review of the CDs led to the selection of one by Bonnie Raitt. Darryl dropped it into the machine, pressed

Play and was halfway across the room before he discovered the disc featured a soprano singing Mozart.

"You like Kathleen Battle, too?" Belle asked.

"I do now." There was no room for him on the couch, so Darryl sat on the floor. It was comfortable on the carpet, and he liked having Belle close by.

At this angle, his head rested lightly against her stomach. It felt good to make casual contact, even without any sexual overtones.

It occurred to Darryl that he ought to tell the truth about the article. He and Belle hadn't exactly become friends, but they were no longer enemies, and he didn't like tricking her.

Most likely, she would understand. On the other hand, she might blow up and kick him out. He decided to wait until a little later that evening rather than spoil their mood. Besides, with his stomach this full, he wasn't sure he could pack a suitcase, let alone drive home.

"Isn't this the most glorious music you've ever heard?" she murmured. "I can't believe Mozart composed as fast as his hand could write. He never made rough drafts. He didn't even need a piano. It was as though he were hearing celestial music."

At that moment, Darryl felt a distinctly uncelestial thump in the vicinity of his temple. He couldn't figure out how Belle had done that with her stomach.

"Next time you need to burp, could you please give me a warning?" he said.

"That wasn't me!" She laughed, and dropped her hand to her abdomen. "It was the baby!"

"The baby?"

"It's kicking." Her face was radiant. "It's the first time I've felt it kick!"

"The baby kicked me?" Darryl found it hard to absorb what had just happened. "It must have heard my voice."

"You hadn't said a thing."

She was right, but he couldn't shake the sense that the baby had known its father was close. "Still, I think it was trying to communicate."

"That's the silliest thing I've heard since...since... What was that band that played L.A. last year, the one that beat their shoes together and snorted through their noses?" she asked.

"I must have missed them," he said. "But getting thumped by the baby—it was magical. Didn't you think so? Didn't it feel magical to you, too?"

He felt a long shudder run through her body. "Absolutely."

"Do you think he'll do it again?"

"I don't know. Usually I just feel faint rumblings. It's the first time she's kicked this hard."

Darryl sat without moving for a long time, but the baby didn't stir again. He remembered his intention of telling Belle about the article, but he no longer wanted to take the risk of being tossed out the door.

Maybe a fetus wouldn't communicate in any formal sense, but Darryl couldn't shake the feeling that it knew he was here. Finally, when he was sure the kid must have gone back to sleep and was on the verge of dozing off himself, he said good-night and staggered to his feet.

Belle didn't answer. From her beatific expression, she might have been lost in thoughts about the child, too, or maybe she was simply absorbed in the music. He supposed the baby, now that it was big enough to interact with its parents, might be able to hear Mozart, too. Darryl made a mental note to play lots of classical composers, and then remembered that he would have a devil of a time finding the right CDs.

Alone in his room, he picked up his notebook and began to write. This time, though, he wasn't recounting

omeone else's bittersweet parenting experiences. He was
escribing how a father feels in the presence of a miracle.

Y THE MIDDLE of December, Belle had to admit that
arryl was earning his keep. On weekends, he brought her
reakfast in bed, and once he indulged her craving for
alty foods by going out to buy pretzels and pickles at
0:00 p.m.

And he obviously loved the baby. That aspect of him
urprised her. He insisted that she let him know when-
ver the baby was moving, and would even abandon a
elevised football game to rush over and place his hand on
er abdomen.

The problem was that she liked the stroking and fon-
ling intended for the baby. She didn't want to relish the
el of Darryl's strong hands on her skin. She wished her
nagination would quit tormenting her with fantasies
bout what might have happened that night they spent
gether.

But she didn't really have to worry, because every time
he thought about responding, a wave of indigestion or a
ick in the ribs came along to distract her. Amazingly,
arryl seemed to accept the fact that mood swings went
ith hormonal changes, and hadn't sought a replay of
eir close encounter in the kitchen.

At the *Just Us* offices, the staff was gearing up for the
larch issue. It had always struck Belle as ironic, the way
ey had to think in terms of spring vacation in mid-
ecember.

And this year they also had to plan for the June open-
g of the mall. Sandra had promised to drop by some-
me during the day to show the staff what she'd been
orking on.

"Have you considered what you're going to do when
e baby's born?" Anita asked that afternoon as she of-
red Belle a plate of Easter cookies. "By the way, these

have peanut butter in them. You aren't allergic to it, are
you?''

"No. And I guess I'll go for natural childbirth." She
picked a pink cookie shaped like a bunny, then took an
egg-shaped one for her baby.

Anita tossed back her dark hair, revealing a pair of
snowflake earrings. "I meant the magazine. You'll have
to take some time off in May, won't you?"

"A few days, maybe." Belle had called a referral service and had obtained the names of licensed day-care
providers, but she wasn't crazy about any of the ones
she'd met so far. "If necessary, Sandra can put in a bit
more time. She *is* the publisher."

"Did someone mention my name?" The hat appeared
in the doorway first, a vast undertaking topped with a tiny
Christmas village and miniature teddy bears. It was so
darling that Belle found it impossible to care whether it
might be tacky.

Into the room strolled Sandra, a portfolio under her
arm and a grin on her face. The teddy bears bowed and
danced as she removed three poster-size sheets and laid
them on the desk. "Here it is, ladies! When Mira sees
these, she'll *beg* us to cosponsor the opening!"

Belle, Anita and Janie, who had followed in Sandra'
wake, gathered around. It was immediately obvious from
the professionalism of the drawing and lettering that their
boss had hired a graphic artist to create the renderings.

At the top of the first poster was the slogan Just Us
Together Into The Future. Below, a drawing of the
planned megamall's vast interior featured manikin families pushing baby carriages and escorting toddlers. Each
wore a T-shirt bearing the slogan.

The second poster depicted the mall's future Cathedral
Court. In the center stood a manikin wedding couple surrounded by their attendants. Above them on the second

floor, "Just Us" was spelled out in red blossoms against white.

The third picture showed a ski scene set up in front of a sporting-goods store, with manikins dressed for the slopes. They were skiing toward a banner that repeated the slogan Just Us: Together Into The Future.

"For the opening, we would place dummies in these tableaux around the mall." Sandra beamed at their impressed reactions. "You know, couples with children, brides and grooms, people enjoying recreational activities. It would make the whole place feel more cozy."

"That's a good motto," Anita said. "It's got this nice chewy texture when I say it, kind of like peanut-butter cookies in my mouth."

Janie nodded. "It's an ongoing fashion show. The merchants can display their wares on the manikins right in the mall. If I were a store owner I'd like that."

They regarded Sandra with new respect. The woman had a real flair for promotion, Belle realized.

"Let's line up a presentation as soon as possible," the publisher said. "*Just Us* is going to cosponsor this mall opening. Right?"

"Right!" they all cheered.

"I'll call now," Belle said, and got on the phone. To her delight, the marketing director promptly gave her a date to make the presentation: January eighth at 1:00 p.m., at the mall's on-site offices.

Hanging up, she relayed the news. The others whooped with excitement.

"Let's celebrate!" Sandra twirled around the room, humming softly. In the teddy bear hat, she resembled a music box come to life. "We need to feel like a team, and what better time for a fresh start than New Year's? I want to invite you—"

She stopped, hands fluttering in midair. "Oh, dear, there's just one thing missing."

"What?" asked Belle.

"We need to know what the other side is planning." Sandra chewed on her lip. "We need a spy at *About Town*. Who could we recruit?"

"Is that ethical?" asked Janie. "I mean, I know you wouldn't do anything unethical, Sandra. I just meant, well, how would it look if anyone found out?"

"Not a spy, exactly," the publisher said. "Just someone who might let a little information slip."

Everyone stared at Belle.

"What?" she said.

"Well, you *are* living with him," said Sandra.

Belle couldn't believe they would ask her to spy on Darryl. She wouldn't and, besides, she couldn't. "He never brings his work home. But..."

Indecisively, she pulled a model's composite photograph from a stack on her desk. It showed Mindy in a variety of poses, wearing different outfits.

"She's done some work for *About Town* and she's very ambitious," Belle said. "She probably drops by their offices fairly often. She came by here yesterday with this."

Sandra took the composite. "I'm inviting you all to my New Year's Eve party." The celebrity-laden event was one of the best-known annual parties in the city. "Maybe this model would like to come, too."

"You think she'd sell out Darryl Horak for an invitation to your party?" Belle asked, feeling both dismay and admiration at such a brash move.

Sandra's party *was* an exciting event. Each time she attended, Belle found herself nearly overwhelmed by the extravagance and the sight of so many famous faces.

"It's worth a try. I'll have some top agents and directors there, you know," said the publisher. "It's a rare opportunity for her."

"In her place, I'd probably go along with it," said Anita. "I mean, she could get rich and famous real quick."

"If she knows anything," cautioned Janie.

Remembering the skittish woman who'd fled on Thanksgiving, Belle actually felt sorry for her. But they weren't asking her to do anything awful, just to describe something she might have seen. It wasn't as if she owed Darryl any loyalty.

I wouldn't tell, if it were me, she thought. But then, Darryl had given her a particularly long back rub the previous night. That called for at least a smidgen of loyalty.

Sandra dialed the phone number on the composite and got an answering service that put her through to Mindy's home. From what Belle could hear of the conversation, it didn't take much tempting. A few minutes later, the publisher hung up, elated.

"She's seen their posters, all right," she announced. "All she would reveal is the theme, but that's helpful."

"Well?" demanded Belle. "What is it?"

"About Town: Adam Brings Eve Back to Paradise," said Sandra.

A chorus of catcalls filled the room.

"Adam *brings* Eve?" demanded Anita. "I wonder if I could throw the rest of my cookies far enough to hit those chauvinists in the head."

"It sounds like something Greg would come up with!" hooted Janie. "Can you believe it? I honestly can't believe they would go that far overboard."

"I can see it now." Sandra, as usual, managed to dominate the room with a mere tilt of her head. "A paradise theme. Women in sarongs and bikinis. Perhaps a man in a tuxedo, James Bond-style. We'll pull the rug right out from under their feet. We'll incorporate a scene just like that."

"Did she by any chance say when they're making their presentation?" Janie asked.

"January eighth," said Sandra. "That isn't—Was that—When did you say we were scheduled, Belle?"

"The same day."

"Probably the same time, too," Sandra said grimly. "Didn't Mira say she likes to get people together to compare ideas?"

"She thinks it generates creativity," Belle recalled.

"It might generate mass murder," grumbled Janie.

"Don't worry, ladies," said Sandra. "I'll take care of this situation. I'm *glad* we'll be seeing Mira at the same time—we can use it to our advantage. And let's all be extra friendly to Mindy at the party. We owe her a great deal."

As the others chorused their agreement, Belle realized what this meant. Mindy would be at the party, with her luscious mane of dark hair and her incredibly willowy body.

Even though Belle's rational mind reminded her that she was carrying a new life, she couldn't help feeling awkward about her lumpish figure. Fancy clothes would only emphasize her rotundness and everyone else's sleekness.

As her houseguest, Darryl would naturally accompany her to Sandra's. The prospect of being contrasted with all those glamorous people was daunting.

Really, she decided, she would rather stay home and be comfortable. There were more enjoyable things to do on New Year's Eve than mingle with famous people and eat fabulous food.

She just wished she could think of what those things were.

9

THE BEACH LAY peaceful in the haze of a December morning. Only a few seals played among the waves. Darryl inhaled the briny air and picked up his pace, the slap of his jogging shoes on the walkway forming a counterpoint to his troubled thoughts.

Belle had slept late, this being Saturday morning. Despite his resolve to wait on her, he hadn't been able to resist sneaking out. He'd needed to pick up mail, and he missed his usual jogging route.

Besides, he was having trouble facing her since turning in his article yesterday. Even though he owed the truth to those unhappy fathers, he couldn't help feeling as if he'd betrayed her trust.

It didn't help that Belle had come home last night looking depressed. It never ceased to surprise Darryl how clearly the woman showed her emotions.

When she was happy, her face glowed. When she was sad, she wilted like a flower.

She'd muttered something about Sandra Duval's New Year's Eve party and how she didn't want to go. Darryl couldn't figure out why not. He would love to attend.

He'd been almost certain the cause of her unhappiness was that he would be going to visit his aunt and uncle in Santa Barbara for Christmas next week, but Belle had declined his invitation to join them. She was looking forward to spending the day with Janie's family in nearby Inglewood, she said.

If the problem wasn't Christmas, what was it? Darryl waved absentmindedly to one of his volleyball buddies as they passed each other, jogging in opposite directions. How was a guy supposed to figure out what went through a woman's mind when she refused to tell him? He wished Belle would spill out her thoughts as clearly as she revealed her emotions.

He was nearing the coffee shop that marked the turning point of his jog when he spotted Jim Rickard. Jim, who earned money between assignments by peddling human-interest pictures to news syndicates, was photographing a toddler feeding a sea gull.

The boy looked a lot like Nick at that age. Tori had recently canceled plans to bring the boy west to visit his father this Christmas, announcing that they would be going to Florida with her new boyfriend instead. Darryl wondered if Jim had been drawn to the toddler because he missed his own son.

Halting beside some parked cars, Darryl jogged in place until his friend finished shooting. Then, by unspoken mutual agreement, they moved along the outer lines of a triangle until they intersected in front of the coffee shop.

"Inside or out?" Jim brushed sand from his jeans.

"Out." Darryl chose a table near the railing that gave them an unobstructed view of the beach. "I've been indoors too much these days."

"How's it going?" asked his friend, straddling a chair across from him.

Darryl explained about completing the article and feeling guilty. "After all, she is having my kid," he said.

Jim, Greg and Elva had all figured out by now that the child was his, and he didn't bother to pretend otherwise. As long as the press didn't find out, Darryl saw no point in keeping his paternity a secret.

"And now she's down in the dumps and I'm not sure why," he concluded as the waitress delivered their cups of cappuccino. "She says she doesn't even want to go to Sandra Duval's New Year's Eve party."

"I don't pretend to be an expert on women," Jim said. "If I were, I'd have been more careful who I married."

"Sandra's famous for laying on a great spread," Darryl continued. "And Belle loves parties."

"Maybe she's avoiding it because pregnant women aren't supposed to drink," Jim suggested.

"So what?" Darryl wasn't much of a drinker himself. He had developed a particular aversion to spiked punch. "I'm sure they'll have soft drinks."

Jim drummed his fingers on the table. "Could there be somebody she wants to avoid?"

"Me," Darryl said. "But she won't know it until the article comes out."

"Then it must be her weight," he said. "Tori refused to go anywhere when she was pregnant. She thought she looked like a cow."

"You mean Belle is pouting because she can't fit into a size seven?" Darryl demanded. "That's ridiculous!"

"Well, perhaps there's something deeper affecting her moods." Jim gazed at the ocean as it swelled with one of its periodic high waves. "Having a baby means her life is changing forever."

"So is mine." Darryl couldn't believe his friend was overlooking the obvious. "As you know, my whole article is about the fact that parenthood means as much to men as to women."

The photographer turned toward him, his gaze locking with Darryl's. "But you're not married to her, my friend. So your life is only changing as much as you want it to."

The comment seemed so blatantly unfair that Darryl couldn't even figure out where to start protesting. In any case, he didn't get a chance, because the wave was subsiding, leaving a dazed-looking seal floundering on the sand.

"I've got to get a shot of that," Jim said as a couple of children approached the seal cautiously. "And make sure the critter gets away safely, of course." He tossed some money on the table. "Happy New Year, my friend."

"Same to you," Darryl said, and meant it.

Jim had been way off base, but he'd only been trying to help.

GIRL, YOU HAVE to get it together. So it's New Year's Eve. So everybody else is going to be eating shrimp and Brie and you'll be chomping chips and watching TV. Who cares?

Belle regarded herself grimly in the bathroom mirror. A red blotch on the side of her nose bore a suspicious resemblance to a zit. She suspected Mindy's skin had been airbrushed at birth. So had everyone else's among the beautiful people of Los Angeles.

Wallowing in self-pity was not productive but it felt good. She was glad that Darryl had gone out earlier so she could indulge herself. She wondered if *An Affair to Remember* would be on cable tonight to give her an excuse for a good cry.

Slouching into the kitchen, she sat at the table and began writing her New Year's resolutions:

No. 1. Throw Darryl out and turn spare bedroom into nursery.

No. 2. Keep Darryl and make him redecorate nursery.

No. 3. Replace Darryl with Brad Pitt.

Hearing a key turn in the outer door, Belle crumpled the list and tossed it in the trash. On a second sheet of paper, she wrote:

No. 1. Reread *War and Peace*.

No. 2. Learn Japanese.

No. 3. Make exercise video.

Darryl came in carrying a large plastic bag. "What are you doing?"

"Making my New Year's resolutions," she said.

To her disappointment, he didn't read over her shoulder. Instead, he handed her the bag, which was draped on a hanger.

"For you," he said.

Belle regarded the gift suspiciously. "What is it?"

"Go put it on." There was a determination in Darryl's tone that made her stand and head for the bedroom. She might as well see what he'd brought, she told herself.

Closing the door behind her, Belle reached inside the plastic covering. Her hand touched something that felt crunchy, the way evening dresses did when they were shot through with glittery threads. Puzzled, she removed the bag and examined the garment.

It was a black dress woven with metallic threads that shifted colors in the lamplight. The tag read One Size Fits All.

Belle couldn't resist. Peeling off her oversize T-shirt and stretch-paneled jeans, she wiggled into it.

The mirror on the back of the door showed a low-cut yoke revealing ample cleavage. Billowing sleeves gathered at the wrist while, below the bust, the dress cascaded to a scarf hemline that teased her calves.

The dark color set off the brilliant red of her hair, which Belle had touched up the previous day in a fit of restlessness. She hated to admit it, but Darryl had found the one dress capable of luring her out of her nest.

From the closet, she retrieved a pair of low-heeled black boots studded with tiny rhinestones. They gave the outfit a distinctive look-at-me note.

As she applied makeup, she refused to ascribe any noble motives to her housemate. Everyone she knew ached to attend Sandra Duval's party. Obviously, it had been worth this investment to Darryl. Still, she was glad he'd made the effort.

She emerged from the bedroom in a burst of goodwill at the same time that Darryl stepped from the spare room. He wore a tuxedo, shiny black with a pleated white shirt. Its tailored lines emphasized his height and masculine build.

In the rough-and-tumble of everyday life, Belle had forgotten how handsome Darryl could be. From his high cheekbones to his confident stance, he radiated sophistication.

He hadn't merely created the *About Town* male for his readers to emulate. He really was that man, and, tonight, he belonged to Belle.

She took his arm and let him lead her out of the condo. For this one occasion, she would indeed let Adam bring Eve to Paradise.

SANDRA'S MANSION LAY in the exclusive community of Bel-Air Estates, just west of Beverly Hills. Tucked among trees and curving roads lay some of the region's most expensive real estate.

Thousands of lights sparkled along the driveway, where uniformed valets were assisting the guests. White bulbs winked from treetops and hedges, turning the scene into a fairyland.

A cluster of paparazzi waited near the street, dodging cars as they snapped the new arrivals. Channel 17 was there too, its minicam sweeping the driveway. Belle gave a little wave and hoped the black gown would disguise the fullness of her waistline.

There was no dragon master with a guest list, but a pleasant-faced attendant who apparently recognized the invitees on sight. He greeted Belle and Darryl warmly, by name.

The grand entryway opened into a living room large enough to serve as a hotel lobby. Beneath an enormous Christmas tree, a tuxedoed musician at a grand piano played something lyrical.

As they made their way between jewel-encrusted guests in designer gowns, Belle noted that the ceiling had been turned into a planetarium of celestial vistas. The party's theme must be outer space.

Everywhere she glanced, she saw some creative touch: a spray of white flowers interspersed with silver planets, a three-tiered tray filled with green cheese, even a life-size tableau of manikin astronauts planting the flag on the moon.

As they reached the French doors leading outside, the piano music was superseded by the infectious Latin rhythms of a dance band. When they stepped over the threshold, the balmy night twinkled with real stars.

In the center of the swimming pool loomed an ice sculpture of the planet Saturn, complete with rings. Sandra had outdone herself.

Belle thought about the megamall presentation scheduled next week and wondered how Darryl imagined he could upstage Sandra Duval. But judging from his admiring smile, that problem hadn't crossed his mind.

Across the water, a pool house with its doors thrown open displayed a series of cloth-covered tables. They held more food than Belle had ever seen outside a supermarket, tiers of canapés and seafood and desserts.

But neither the decor nor the catering could overshadow the guests. She recognized many of her favorite movie and television stars, rock singers and even a few politicians.

It had been foolish to worry about the contrast between her figure and Mindy's. When they spotted the model, she simply blended into the general feminine swirl of aerobicized and liposuctioned perfection.

At the pool house, Sandra waved cheerily from where she stood in a knot of male admirers. Or gold diggers. Sandra had confessed once that she never expected to marry again, because there was no one she could trust to love her for herself.

Belle decided that inheriting fifty million dollars would make it worth having that kind of problem.

She picked among the shrimp and crab but didn't have much appetite. Mostly, she kept noticing Darryl.

Everything about him bristled with aristocratic self-possession, even the way he scooped up caviar on a cracker. He moved along the main buffet table as if it, and the rest of the world, belonged to him.

Yet tonight she couldn't resent him. He was too essential, too primitive. At this party, the man was in his element, and Belle was glad she'd agreed to come.

Their gazes met over a stuffed mushroom. One eyebrow quirked, and Darryl tossed down the canapé and left his plate on the table.

Moving to Belle's side, he murmured, "Would you care to dance?"

The music had changed to a vibrant rock tune. "Sure," she said.

Globes of light, like those that had swept ballrooms of the Big Band era, dappled the dance floor set up on a stretch of lawn beyond the swimming pool. Only a handful of couples were gyrating on the smooth wooden planking.

Belle's shoulders and hips began to quiver in time to the music. Before she knew it, the rhythm had propelled her into the middle of the dance floor.

Darryl was right there beside her, in front of her, behind her. Laughing. Spinning her around. Raking her with appreciative glances.

There was nothing intimate about their contact, yet she felt aware of him in a new way. She always sensed where he was, and he possessed an almost magical ability to support her without missing a step.

On its platform, the band segued into a cha-cha. Darryl caught Belle and they executed the steps together, so caught up in their enjoyment that they were scarcely aware of the admiration of the onlookers.

She had never felt so comfortable in anyone's arms. They were completely in sync. This was something that only happened between a couple who knew each other intimately. Her body, it seemed, remembered things her brain could not.

The tempo slowed. A female singer with a low, smoky voice began to croon of hopeless love and endless desire.

Darryl's grasp shifted until he cradled Belle against him. Her cheek pressing into his shoulder, she inhaled the deep male essence of him.

From an unseen garden drifted the fragrance of exotic flowers, enveloping them in a sensuous cocoon. She lost all consciousness of the other guests. The two of them might as well have been dancing alone in the Garden of Eden.

Gliding across the floor, she could feel every twitch of Darryl's muscular legs, every shift of his hips. The cool air could no longer dispel the heat radiating from her body.

This couldn't be her. Belle Martens did not live in a fantasy world, nor did she exude hunger and sexual excitement on a dance floor. Most of all, Belle Martens could not be falling in love with Darryl Horak.

The thought nearly stopped her, but it was too late. Her heart defied her brain, refusing to yield the magic of this moment.

Just for a little longer, she would let herself drift through an alternate reality. Just for the space of a song, Belle could fall in love.

DARRYL'S REASON FOR attending this party had been to network. The entire Hollywood A-list was here.

He'd spotted an action-hero whom *About Town* had been seeking to interview for months. By the pool, a trendy new menswear designer from Italy was holding court. His latest collection ought to be a four-page spread for the April issue.

Darryl didn't care.

Between the tall, anorexic beauties, Belle flourished like a lily among reeds. He'd felt vitality and exuberance thrumming through her from the moment they'd arrived.

Maybe it was because she carried new life. Maybe it was simply her personality. Whatever the source, it made Darryl feel as if he had stepped into a different and more wondrous universe.

From this fresh perspective, he could see that the glamour of the other ladies lay skin-deep. While they posed and preened, Belle plunged herself heart and soul into this moment, this dance.

He didn't merely want to make love to her. He wanted to watch her response as he roused her to uncontrollable desire. His own satisfaction was no longer the goal. They had to find ecstasy together.

When the music changed to a faster but still sultry beat, he refused to relinquish her. Belle made no move to pull away, merely quickened her pace to match his.

But inevitably the dance floor began to fill up. Darryl had to focus on avoiding collisions, and then the band switched to a raucous rock number and the spell was broken.

He and Belle wandered back to the pool house. Along the way, they chatted with people they knew, and people they wanted to know, and people who wanted to know them. Afterward, he could barely recall any of their names.

It was only a quarter past eleven when Belle began yawning. Mothers-to-be needed a lot of sleep, Darryl supposed. Besides, after thirty-three years, he no longer found it unthinkable to leave a New Year's Eve party before midnight.

As they drove away from the lights and music, the night lay quiet before them. Other neighborhoods might resound with noisemakers, but not elegant Bel-Air.

In the passenger seat, Belle leaned back, her eyelids drifting shut. Darryl wondered at her ability to stimulate him the way she had earlier. He would never understand this power a woman had, to turn a man twice her size into a lump of longing.

But he needed to get her home and let her rest. Becoming a father sometimes meant putting your woman's and child's needs ahead of your own. It wasn't an easy lesson for him to master, but he was doing his best.

BELLE COULD SENSE Darryl withdrawing. She told herself it was for the best, but she missed their closeness on the dance floor.

She hadn't really fallen in love with him, of course. It had been a dream, a fantasy. But that didn't mean she had to release the enchantment right away. She closed her eyes and imagined they were sailing through the stars.

When they arrived at the condo, her legs felt wobbly. It must be from dancing while carrying the baby's extra weight. Four and a half months of pregnancy might not sound advanced, but on Belle's short frame, it felt like a lot.

In the living room, she got as far as the couch and then sank down. Unwilling to stir, she didn't object when Darryl sat beside her and switched on the TV.

The crowd in Times Square was getting warmed up. "Isn't there anything local?" she asked.

He flipped through the channels. On a news program, they saw shots of people arriving at Sandra Duval's party, and Belle glimpsed the two of them, nearly lost among all those lights. Darryl looked heartbreakingly elegant in his tuxedo, she thought, and was grateful that her dark dress made her figure impossible to see.

She didn't want the night to be over. Not that she regretted leaving. It wasn't the glitz she missed, but that sense of entering into a special, private realm that existed just for the two of them.

Then a commercial came on, and Darryl started clicking again. They passed talk shows, reruns of "Star Trek" and an old TV-movie about a woman suffering from amnesia.

"I always thought they made up that stuff," Belle said. "You know, about people forgetting things. But I swear I can't remember anything that happened that night we got drugged. Can you?"

"I'm still drawing a blank." Darryl stretched his tuxedo-clad legs across the carpet. "But I just thought of a way we might be able to recover our memories."

"What's that?"

He scooted closer and tipped one finger beneath her chin. "By reenacting the events," he said. "Like this."

His mouth closed over Belle's, and before she could stop to think, her arms wound around his neck and she was kissing him back.

She knew this was not a good idea. She also knew that wild and previously unsuspected impulses were racing through her as Darryl probed her lips.

"Are you remembering anything?" he whispered, lifting his head.

"Not yet." She didn't mean to encourage him, but she had to tell the truth, didn't she?

"I think we should pursue this in a logical manner," he said.

There was nothing logical about the sensations tingling across her skin. "How?"

He clicked off the TV just as the fireworks exploded. They were nothing compared to what was happening in this room, she thought.

"Normally, I would begin by kissing you," he said.

"We've done that," she reminded him.

His tongue tapped the edges of his teeth as he considered. They were nice teeth, white and even, Belle thought. "Maybe we should just let our instincts take over."

He was teasing her, of course. He didn't care about recovering his memory any more than she did. He was just taking their intimacy on the dance floor to the next, irresistible level.

And she wanted him to. For one night, Belle ached to yield to the crazy, hopeless, overwhelming impulse to fall in love. Darryl was the wrong man for her, and this enchantment wouldn't last any longer than star shine and dance music, but she wanted to experience every delirious moment.

This time, she knew, she would hold the memory inside her forever.

"So tell me," she whispered. "What do your instincts tell you to do?"

He slipped one arm behind her back and kissed her again for a very long time. His other hand stroked her

cheek, then traveled down her throat to the valley between her breasts.

Belle's entire nervous system might have been wired to
those twin points of her anatomy. Her nipples grew taut
and hot lava spread through her marrow.

Darryl eased the dress off one shoulder, lowering the
bra strap with it. He leaned down and his tongue traced
the edge of one nipple.

A moan twisted from her throat and her back arched in
instinctive feminine invitation. She could feel herself losing control. It had never happened to her before—and yet
it had.

Vaguely, she recalled experiencing this wild urge to join
with a creature of the night. It must have been in a dream,
or, rather, in a drug-enhanced state. There had been a
wolf stalking her, a wolf that transformed itself into a man
of mist and magic.

He was here now. He was Darryl.

As he lowered her across the couch, Belle thought she
remembered the sure strokes of his hands smoothing away
her dress, but she couldn't be sure. And it no longer mattered.

10

SHE ENCIRCLED DARRYL with her arms, probing the expanse of his back. His muscles rippled as her hands explored down his narrow waist and along his hips.

The man quivered, and she felt the pressure of his knee parting her legs. His tuxedo brushed over her bare skin, silky and rough at the same time.

Taking a long breath, Darryl elevated himself and tore away his garments like a feral creature casting off civilization. In the ferocity of his gaze, Belle saw wonder and joy and a deep, driving hunger.

Their mouths came together again, hers yielding, his demanding. His chest crushed her breasts, and she urged him on with long caresses.

He shifted her on the couch, positioning her to receive him. Belle knew what was coming, but she knew it from a dream, an impossible experience in which she had merged with a beast from her darkest fantasies.

Darryl entered her slowly, every inch of him a longed-for intrusion. They fused moment by moment, in an almost unbearable suspension of nature's promptings.

Then he was deep inside her, and she could hold out no longer. Her pelvis began to rotate, teasing him until he burst into a series of hard thrusts.

Cries rasped from his throat. Belle wanted to delay, but the fierceness of his assault left no room for escape. Waves of pleasure burst through her core, and nothing existed in the world but Darryl's conquest and her triumph.

The fire died slowly to embers. He lay half over her and half beside her, breathing heavily. "I'm still not sure," he said.

"What?" She couldn't grasp his meaning.

"I'm not sure whether I remember." A smile dawned on his face. "I guess we'll have to do it again."

So they did.

BELLE WOKE UP the next morning with a sense of unreality. She couldn't have made love with Darryl last night, could she? It must be another of those disappointing dreams in which she started to recall their drugged night together and then awoke to find herself alone.

She rolled over and examined the figure beside her. He looked much as he had that first morning, one arm thrown over his eyes to block the light, his broad chest exposed.

It amazed her that where once she had seen only flaws and annoyances, now she found herself craving the sound of his voice and the glint of his smile. For one aching moment, Belle admitted she felt a deep bond to this man.

Never before had she cared this much about anyone. In the past, she had kept men at bay, reluctant to risk getting hurt. She wouldn't have allowed it now, but Darryl and circumstances had conspired against her.

He had penetrated her defenses so thoroughly, she wasn't sure how she would recover, or if she could. His masculine scent tantalized her, and the sight of his rumpled dark hair brought back memories of exquisite pleasure.

She ran her hand lightly across his skin. This time, she wasn't wondering how it would feel to get intimate with some male model. She was remembering every tantalizing detail of the night before.

And, just as he had that first morning, Darryl reacted with a spurt of energy. Before Belle could respond, she found the man on top of her, his mouth on her breasts and his leg teasing hers apart.

Then he stopped.

"Go on," Belle said.

Dazed brown eyes blinked down at her. "Pain," he said.

"What's wrong?"

"Isn't this the point where you bit me?"

She chuckled. "That was then. This is now."

Darryl gave a long sigh. "Give me a few minutes. My libido just fled in terror."

Before it could return, however, they both decided they were hungry. After showering and breakfasting on toast with marmalade, they faced their first day as lovers.

"Is it okay if I watch the Rose Parade?" Darryl asked.

"You don't need permission," she said. "You live here."

"I just wondered what *you* wanted to do."

"The Rose Parade sounds like fun." And it was.

Still, by the time they had seen most of the floats, Belle was getting edgy. "I think I'll call around and see if any furniture stores are open. I've been meaning to get some bookshelves."

Darryl eyed her makeshift arrangement of cinder blocks. "Any particular style?"

"Whatever catches my eye." She pried herself from the couch. "Any suggestions?"

"I've been thinking of taking up carpentry," he said. "It's kind of a daddy thing. I could borrow a saw from my friend Jim. I mean, I took shop in school, and it can't be that hard to build bookshelves, right?"

Encouraging the man would be a recipe for disaster. With his refusal to consult directions, he was likely to make something even worse than what she had now. "I'll start with one of the malls," Belle said. "The furniture stores are overpriced but they'll probably be open on a holiday. Want to come?"

His fingers twitched as if missing the feel of a saw and some lumber. Then he grinned. "Let's go."

FOR THE NEXT few days at work, it took all Belle's energy just to read copy, deal with free-lancers and check over the magazine as it moved through the process of getting edited. Half the time, Tom in traffic had to remind her that she was due in a meeting, or hadn't revised a caption.

Fortunately, Sandra continued to take the lead on polishing their megamall presentation. Belle's contribution consisted mostly of saying "sure" and "that's terrific" and "what?"

She tried to keep her thoughts from straying to Darryl, but it was difficult. She'd never imagined that lovemaking could be this creative. During the past week, they had initiated the kitchen, the hallway and the bathtub.

He claimed to keep forgetting whether they'd done it before. She pretended to believe him.

This couldn't really be love, of course, not the kind that deepened and lasted through the years, Belle kept reminding herself. She knew better than to expect the impossible. But how many lives were touched by this kind of magic, even for a while?

New Year's Day, when they'd gone shopping, they hadn't bought any bookshelves, but they'd had fun looking in windows and browsing through bookstores. Darryl could be a lot of fun, when he wasn't driving her crazy.

On the morning of January eighth, she awoke with the nervous sense that something important was about to happen. Then she remembered that she and Darryl would be going to the megamall today. Their presentations had, as Sandra'd predicted, both been scheduled for the same time.

Staggering down the hall, she saw him standing in front of the spare bedroom, gazing into it. "Is something wrong?"

"Do they make wallpaper with baseball players on it?" he asked.

Belle could feel herself starting to bristle. "I told you, I'm painting the nursery purple."

He slanted her a grin that was much too alert for this hour of the morning. "I was thinking of a strip of wallpaper around the top."

"Tennis might be all right," she said.

"Really?" he asked. "You're willing to consider a sports motif?"

"As long as there are women players, too." Belle yawned. "How can you worry about something like this today?"

"The baby's first impressions could be important," Darryl said. "Hey, you're not nervous, are you? About the presentations?"

She rubbed a sleeper from her eye. "A little, I guess." She wondered how he would react when he discovered that his theme had been one-upped.

"What's done is done," Darryl told her. "We've got our presentations ready. Now it's up to Ms. Lemos."

"You sound so blasé!" she teased. "I'll bet you're a quivering lump of jelly inside."

"Yeah? Lump of jelly or not, I'll bet I can get dressed before you can!"

"No fair!" she protested as he disappeared into the spare bedroom, where he still kept his clothes even though he no longer slept there. When he failed to respond, Belle slogged the rest of the way to the bathroom.

She emerged from the shower to find Darryl standing before her wearing a dark three-piece suit. He examined her body with interest. "Is that how you're going to the mall? It should make quite an impression."

"I'm illustrating our theme," Belle retorted. "'Just Us: Naked As Nature Intended.'"

His hands cupped her breasts. "Now that *will* catch the public's attention. It's certainly caught mine."

She angled away, laughing. "Too bad we both have to get to the office."

His lips pursed speculatively. "You know, we're expected to ride out to the desert with our colleagues, but we could drive home together. I know a romantic hotel where we could eat a leisurely lunch and have, well, a spectacular dessert."

"That sounds like a plan," said Belle, and shooed him out.

FROM THE ROAD, the High Desert Megamall appeared as an enormous array of linked buildings, sand-colored with hints of sunset pinks and greens. Darryl could hardly tell where it ended and the sky began.

As he pulled into the unpaved parking lot, he was impressed by the sheer size of the place. By June, it would contain a thousand-seat concert hall, movie screens, arcades, a supermarket, seven major department stores and hundreds of shops, along with a hotel, a skating rink and enough restaurants to feed half of California.

He hadn't been entirely honest with Belle this morning. Although he tried to take a fatalistic attitude, Darryl cared very much about landing this account. He was tired of the peeling paint and stained curtains at his office, and the computer equipment needed an upgrade.

On the other hand, he hoped she understood that this was just business. There was no reason this rivalry should interfere with the rapport the two of them had established.

Just the thought of her made heat flood through his veins. It wasn't just her sensuality but the spice of her personality that excited him. Something special happened when two enemies became lovers, and he was sure it could only get better.

Nearby, Elva's Bronco halted and she retrieved some posters from her back seat. Greg emerged from the passenger side carrying a briefcase and, like the brave band of musketeers, the three of them marched toward double glass doors crisscrossed with masking tape.

Inside, the sound of construction filled the vast arched space. Carpenters were at work everywhere, turning cavelike openings into shops.

Skirting piles of sawdust and lumber, Darryl escorted his team to a private elevator, as per Mira's directions. It carried them to the third-floor executive offices.

They stepped into an office still lacking carpet and drapes. From the unusual layout and curving entryways, though, Darryl could see that the place would be impressive once it was finished.

A secretary waved them into a conference room. A check of his watch showed them to be fifteen minutes early, and he was pleased to see that the *Just Us* team hadn't arrived yet. Going first meant hitting the promotions director while she was fresh and, hopefully, more receptive.

Mira popped in a moment later, her dark hair drawn back in a French twist. Shaking hands, she said, "Shall we get down to business?"

On a series of easels, Elva set out her posters. Each illustrated the theme of "Adam Brings Eve Back to Paradise," which would be presented through fashion shows ongoing during the opening weekend.

One section of the mall would feature reggae music and a tropical garden motif; another, country music and sporting gear in an Alpine setting; and a third would present folk music, with merchandise for children displayed in a fairy-tale village. Each show, as depicted in the posters, included a disappointed-looking serpent hissing as Adam rehooked an apple to its tree.

The key, in Darryl's opinion, was the thematic reference to Adam and Eve. Its emphasis on masculine responsibility summarized all that was controversial and up-to-the-minute about the proposal and would make the mall stand out in consumers' minds.

"The point we'll be making throughout our magazine over the next few months," he said, "is that the nineties are the years of commitment. We'll be encouraging men to reassert their importance in the family."

Mira studied the posters, but revealed nothing of her reaction. The absence of a response made him uneasy. If she had fallen in love with the presentation, she would surely be showing it by now.

It was almost a relief to hear voices outside and realize the *Just Us* crew had landed. He could only hope that they'd come up with something so cozy and domestic that his offering would shine by comparison.

Into the room breezed Sandra Duval, wearing a broad-brimmed hat covered with little hearts and cupids like a harbinger of Valentine's Day. Belle and two of her staff members followed.

They were all smiling. Perversely, Darryl couldn't wait to see them get shot down. Misery loved company, he supposed.

Then Janie Frakes's grin disappeared as her eyes met Greg's. The two glared briefly before averting their gazes. They must have strong feelings for each other to maintain a feud this long, Darryl mused.

Sandra finished shaking hands with Ms. Lemos while her staff festooned the room with posters. The theme, "Just Us: Together into the Future," was about what Darryl had expected. He definitely preferred "Naked As Nature Intended."

He wasn't surprised by the manikin families pushing their babies through the mall. He was bored by the manikin wedding scene, although Mira studied it with interest.

At the third panel, "Just Us Tonight!" Darryl squirmed. The men and women in sophisticated evening dress were poaching on *About Town* territory.

He'd assumed all along that there would be an evening-wear fashion show but hadn't thought to depict it. Before he could point this out, however, Sandra set up the last poster, "Just Us in Paradise."

The scene virtually duplicated Elva's poster of a couple in swimsuits romancing each other in a tropical garden. Worse, the pair were playing catch with apples, as if to burlesque the whole Adam and Eve theme. Darryl could almost have sworn Belle had read his notes, except that he'd been careful not to take anything home with him.

Mira nodded in appreciation as she regarded the display. Greg stared at it irritably. In Elva's clenched teeth and narrowed eyes, Darryl saw a fury that matched his own.

Sandra explained her theme in a breathless voice. The woman managed to lend an air of careless worldliness to everything she did, and today she was at her best.

Darryl's spirits plummeted. He couldn't believe they might lose.

"This is fascinating," said Mira, which was more encouragement than she'd given *About Town*.

Belle chewed on her lower lip. If she had won fair and square, she should be beaming. To Darryl's critical gaze, she appeared downright guilty.

Elva must have noticed the same thing. "They cheated," she whispered in Darryl's ear. "I don't know how they did it, but they've been snooping. Well, they can't get away with this."

"Wait a minute." He wasn't sure he liked the sound of that. "What are you planning to—?"

From her briefcase, Elva whipped a preliminary print-out of the March issue, including the cover, and announced in her loudest voice, "Ms. Lemos, we're going to be generating a lot of controversy with our March issue and we think the High Desert Megamall should take advantage of it, since it dovetails with our theme. Here's an advance look at what I'm talking about."

As Mira accepted the pages, Sandra peeked over her shoulder. "'The Natural Superiority of Men As Parents,'" she read, all wide-eyed innocence. "Oh, how interesting! Can men get pregnant now?"

"May I have a look at that?" asked Belle as the marketing director finished scanning the printout.

Darryl's instincts screamed to yank the pages from Mira's hands and flee, but he couldn't do that. This was business.

Besides, Belle would find out sooner or later. He'd simply been hoping it would be later.

Mira, Sandra and Elva filled the air with chatter that might have been in Swahili for all Darryl cared. His attention was riveted on Belle.

As she read the feature article, her face went white. He wondered which part offended her most, the fact that he'd lied to her or the sheer effrontery of his theme, and then realized that it made no difference.

While writing it, he had been absorbed with the idea of doing justice to Jim and the other fathers. He had assumed that Belle would understand the need for exaggeration, as well as the inclusion of a few humorous details about her morning sickness and weight gain.

Observing her shocked expression, he suddenly viewed the article from a different perspective. He had moved into Belle's condo on false pretenses and spied on her most intimate behavior, then subjected her to public ridicule.

Even though he hadn't named her, plenty of people would guess the truth.

A deep and unfamiliar sensation called shame spread through Darryl's gut. He had hurt Belle and betrayed her confidence. At that moment, he would have given anything to go back in time and reverse his own actions.

She said nothing. The silence, so unlike Belle, was disturbing.

"I do find your magazine interesting, as well as both your presentations." Mira studied both sets of poster-size drawings. "I have to admit, there are elements in each that appeal to me."

"But ours is the superior one, wouldn't you agree?" said Sandra.

Mira didn't take the bait. "I had given some thought to linking up with a bridal magazine. You know the one, *Flowers and Lace?*"

A chorus of indrawn breaths and murmurs of "Not that!" greeted this painful revelation.

"But it is rather limiting," the promotions director went on. "I'd like for your two magazines to get together on this. One appeals mostly to men, the other to women. I'd like to see a unified theme. Be sure to keep the wedding scene as a climax."

"We couldn't possibly work together!" It was the first remark Belle had made since seeing the article.

Her publisher favored the room with a vague smile, as if her editor must have been joking. "If we agree to do that, can we count on your approval?" she asked Mira. "We've already put in quite a few hours. We couldn't possibly do any more work on speculation."

The woman was smarter than Darryl had given her credit for. While the rest of them stood around like stunned cattle, Sandra was closing the deal.

Mira surveyed the posters. "Yes, all right. You both agree?"

"Sure." Darryl wasn't sure where the voice came from, but it sounded like his.

"Absolutely," said Sandra.

Belle stood motionless. He needed to talk with her, so he caught her arm and led her out of the conference room before she could protest.

11

BELLE SAID NOTHING all the way down in the elevator. It wasn't until they approached his car that she spoke.

"I'm not riding with you."

Darryl held the door open. "Would you rather have this conversation now or later?"

After a moment's hesitation, she got in the car. She still didn't meet his gaze.

He decided she might feel better if he left the first move to her. They had a two-hour drive, which would give her time to collect herself before broaching the subject.

They were approaching the exit to the parking lot when she said, "You can move out this afternoon or tonight, whichever you prefer."

She couldn't mean it. "Why don't we wait until you calm down before we make any decisions?"

"I am calm, regardless of what you may think of my hormonal state," growled Belle. "You moved in to research your article. You've done that. Boy, have you done that! I would never have treated you that way, never!"

Her eyes glittered suspiciously. It hurt him to realize she was on the verge of tears. The damn article wasn't worth it.

"I just wasn't thinking," he said. "My focus was on fathers who've been deprived of their children."

"You said you were writing an article sympathetic to women," Belle said grimly.

"I'm sorry." It sounded inadequate, but Darryl meant it. "Things have changed between us this past week. It was too late to stop the article. Surely you can give me a second chance."

"No," she said.

"No? That's it?"

"That's it."

"What about the nursery?" He knew it wasn't a key point, but he couldn't think of anything else. "I was going to put up wallpaper."

"I'll do it myself."

"You're too short. It will snap down and roll you into a ball and they'll find you three days later in convulsions from sugar withdrawal." The freeway must be around here somewhere, but was it to the left or the right?

"If you don't move out, I'll change the locks and you can claim your belongings at the Lost and Found," she snapped. "Or maybe the animal shelter."

He took a blind guess and turned left. "Belle, I know I invaded your privacy, and I'm sorry. I was beginning to think maybe the two of us had a future together. I still think so, if you'll only be reasonable."

"Reasonable?" she said. "How can I be? Everybody who read your article knows that pregnant women make mountains out of molehills. We're a seething mass of hysteria."

"I didn't mean to make fun of you." Gratefully, he noticed a freeway sign ahead. "I'm sorry this turned out so badly. Let's at least agree to stay friends, for our baby's sake."

She shook her head tightly. "I can manage alone, thank you."

Her words sent a chill through him. "I'm not going to fade into the sunset. I love that kid, Belle. You can't throw me out of his life."

"Can't I?" she retorted. "You've been playing at fatherhood. To you, this is all one big political point to make in your magazine." Tears spilled over, but she ignored them. "You have no right to this child, Darryl Horak. I'm taking full responsibility."

He felt as if someone had knocked the wind out of him. In his sympathy for Jim and the fathers' group, Darryl had never imagined that he might find himself shut out of his child's life. "Whether you like it or not, this is my baby, too," he said. "If you won't share, I'm suing for custody."

The moment the words flew out, he regretted them. Yet how could he back off? He couldn't force Belle to forgive him, but he wouldn't allow her to deprive their child of a father.

Her jaw dropped. When she clamped it shut an instant later, there was a steely determination in her jawline that he hadn't seen before.

He'd gone too far, Darryl realized. He didn't intend to take the child away. He just wanted to stay close.

"We can work this out," he said. "Belle? Talk to me."

She pulled a tissue from her purse and blew her nose, but there were no more words all the way to Los Angeles.

As they exited the freeway, Darryl said, "Let's go home and talk. We shouldn't leave things up in the air."

"I have work to do." The statement came out low and tense.

"This is more important."

"Are you kidnapping me?"

"Of course not." Arguing was useless while she remained in this mood, Darryl decided, and reluctantly dropped her at her office.

BELLE HARDLY NOTICED the happy buzz of conversation as the rest of the staff celebrated their cosponsorship of the megamall. Having to share it with *About Town* was only a minor liability, in everyone's opinion except hers.

How could she concentrate on her work, knowing Darryl was plotting to take the baby away? Okay, she conceded silently, maybe he wasn't actually plotting, but there was no way to be sure.

She'd trusted him when he'd moved into her condo, and all along he'd been using her. The thought of how intimate they'd become hurt deeply. The scent of him lingered on her clothing, and several times she thought she heard his voice calling her before she remembered that she was at work.

What if he really did sue for custody? With that article about deprived fathers stirring up public sympathy, he might even win.

She needed to get public opinion on her side. Was it possible Channel 17 might take an interest in reviving the scandal about the drugged punch?

An unintended pregnancy, a rivalry that was exploding into a custody battle.... Belle hated to think about the invasion of her privacy. But hadn't Darryl gone public by writing his article?

An ache swelled inside at the memory of how he'd looked on New Year's Day when they'd awakened together. And how much fun they'd had browsing through malls, and how they'd discovered this past week that they both enjoyed archeology programs on cable TV. She had actually begun to believe that the two of them might belong together.

But love had to be based on trust. How could he have made love to her, and pretended to care about her, when all the while he was simply researching an article at her expense?

Biting back tears, Belle picked up the phone.

As HE DROVE HOME that night, Darryl braced himself to make further apologies. Surely her anger would have grown cold by now.

His confidence faded, however, as he noticed his suitcase sitting on Belle's porch. Even before he tried to fit his key into the lock, an instinct told him it wouldn't fit.

It didn't.

Worst of all was the note. It said: "D. Watch the Channel 17 News at ten o'clock."

He didn't want to face this alone, so as soon as he got home, he invited Greg over to watch with him. They fixed themselves a snack and sat down to watch the news. "I hope they put the sports on first," Greg said.

"I hope we have a massive power failure," said Darryl.

They got neither. Right after the headline stories, the anchorman and anchorwoman reminded viewers about last September's tale of spiked punch and the speculation concerning the two rival editors.

"Kate Munro has an update for us," said the anchorwoman. "Kate?"

The face of the reporter dominated the screen. "I'm here at the offices of *Just Us* magazine with Belle Martens. She has quite an announcement for us. Belle?"

The camera pulled back to show a woebegone woman in an old-fashioned sailor dress, her defiant red hair tucked beneath a scarf.

"She looks seduced and abandoned," said Greg.

That, Darryl gathered, was the idea.

Belle faced the camera. "I'm pregnant. The father is Darryl Horak and it happened after we both drank spiked punch at a party. It was an accident. It wasn't Darryl's fault or mine."

"What made you decide to go public?" Kate asked.

"Darryl Horak is trying to exploit my baby," she said. First he moved in with me under the pretext of re-

searching an article sympathetic to mothers. Instead, he
wrote a story attacking motherhood and invading my
privacy. Now he's threatening to sue for custody! All he
really cares about are fame and money.''

''That's me—rich and famous,'' Darryl grumbled.
What a mess! His hope of reaching a discreet under
standing was diminishing with every word she spoke on
the air.

And he missed Belle. Even though he knew she had as
sumed an air of pathos for public-relations purposes, he
ached to comfort and reassure her.

''We're glad you let us tell your side of the story,'' Kate
said. ''Of course, you understand, we have to give Mr.
Horak equal time if he requests it.''

Dismay flashed across Belle's face. Apparently she
hadn't given much thought to the public battle she might
be unleashing.

As the camera cut away, Darryl realized he didn't have
much choice. He couldn't allow Belle to cut him off from
the baby, and he didn't like being portrayed as a heartless
predator.

He didn't want to attack her, either. He just wanted to
make the point that kids needed fathers, too. ''I suppose
I'll have to go on the air myself.''

Greg nodded. ''Never let a woman get the better of you.
You know, I'm really sorry that I ran around on Janie.
She's a special lady. But I can't let her know that or she'd
wipe the floor with me.''

''You ought to apologize,'' Darryl said.

''Oh?'' asked his friend. ''Is that what you're going to
do?''

''More or less,'' Darryl answered.

''WE NEED AN ANGLE,'' Belle told her staff as they sa
around the *Just Us* boardroom examining the almost

finished March edition of the magazine. "This is great, and I like our April theme, but May needs punching up."

March's pages had been laser-printed and pasted onto flat boards for final inspection. The key people were here—Tom from traffic, the advertising director, Janie, Anita, Belle and Sandra—all searching for errors.

They were also taking advantage of the meeting to look ahead. This month's theme, "Forget Thin—Think Healthy!" was a hit with the staff. Work was under way on April's issue, based on an idea from Janie: "The Future Starts Here! How to Get a Better Job and a Better Love Life!"

But nobody was enthusiastic about May's proposed theme of "Be Ready for the Greatest Summer Ever!" They needed something snappier, preferably a theme that made women feel good about themselves.

Belle felt as if she'd struck a blow for women when she'd appeared on Channel 17 the previous week. The only problem was that, after the station's open invitation to Darryl, she kept feeling as if she were waiting for him to respond.

Of course he would try to get back at her, wouldn't he? She couldn't help replaying their conversation in the car, when he'd actually apologized. And he'd mentioned something about a future together.

Surely she had misunderstood. Darryl couldn't really care about her. He couldn't be feeling the same hollowness every day when he ate breakfast alone, and every evening when he came home to an empty apartment.

"Belle?" asked Janie. "What's wrong? You've hardly said a word."

"I'm worried about Darryl," she admitted.

"Horak?" asked Sandra, as if there were any other Darryls in Belle's life. "I hear he's going to be on the news again tonight."

Her breath caught in her throat. "He is?"

"Going to strike another blow for poor helpless fathers, no doubt," said Anita. "I suppose he has some good points, but—"

"It's so unfair!" Belle burst out. "I don't even have a coach for childbirth classes, while he's going to tell the world what a great dad he is!"

"Childbirth classes?" asked the publisher. "What exactly do they teach you?"

"How to breathe," Janie explained.

"She already knows how to breathe!" Sandra said. "There, you see, Belle? You don't need a coach. Rewrite that headline, would you, dear? It's confusing. Then I think we can let this one go."

"Sure." It was a relief to get back to work.

When Belle returned home at six o'clock, the night air was chilly. Walking from her car to the condo, she found herself listening for familiar masculine footsteps that never came.

Irrationally, she missed Darryl. She wanted him to help cook dinner, to rub her back, to put a CD on the player and then laugh when it turned out to be the wrong one.

As she opened the door, she missed the way his face always lit up when she entered a room. She would never see that look again. The realization left a gray, dismal feeling.

Inside, a faint fragrance lingered. It was a mixture of after-shave lotion, wine and *essence de Darryl*. Maybe an exterminator could get rid of it, she told herself grimly.

As she ate a frozen dinner, she could feel the baby start wiggling. A little foot or an elbow prodded her ribs, then executed a one-two punch that stopped just short of being painful.

That was a small person in there, someone whose genes carried characteristics of Belle's parents and grandparents. It was a link in a chain that had begun in the mist of time, connecting her to ancestors she had never thought about before.

The baby was linked to Darryl's ancestors, too. He would have enjoyed running his hand across her abdomen and feeling the restless movements.

Maybe she was wrong to try to close him out. If only he hadn't threatened to sue for custody!

A tiny hope was born inside her, that on the news tonight he would tell the world he had no intention of trying to take away this baby. Then maybe they could be friends again.

She really could use his help. After she'd told her parents about the pregnancy a few days ago, Belle had hoped they would offer to stay with her in May when the baby was born.

Instead, her mother had explained that her sister, Bari, was expecting a baby in July. After two years of infertility treatments, she'd finally become pregnant again but was having problems.

Bari had to stay in bed until her due date. She needed her parents there to watch four-year-old Mikki, and of course they'd agreed.

Belle wanted everything to turn out well for her sister. She had called Bari immediately afterward to offer best wishes. But she felt awfully far away from her family right now.

The scary part was that when she thought of the word *family,* Darryl came to mind. Well, she would just have to watch and listen to what he had to say.

She clicked on the TV and collapsed onto the couch. After a few minutes, the Channel 17 news team announced they had Darryl Horak's response to Belle's announcement about her pregnancy.

Her hands twisted in her lap. *Say the right thing. I don't know what that might be, but you're the one who did me wrong, so it's up to you to find it.*

On camera, Kate Munro and Darryl stood in his living room. Or what used to be his living room. Now wood chips littered newspapers spread on the floor, while a power saw lay on the couch.

"What are you building?" asked the reporter, standing at a safe distance.

Belle's heart leapt. He was making her a bookcase—a peace offering. But her hopes were dashed with his next words.

"A crib!" Darryl indicated a skimpy framework of boards. "I'm just getting started, as you can see. We'll be running a series of articles in *About Town* for fathers on how to build things, how to be your kids' soccer coach, how to take them camping—you know, the stuff dads do best."

As he spoke, he ran one hand along the crib's railing. The structure shuddered. With a stiff smile at the camera, Darryl gripped the railing to steady it.

"I'm not putting my baby in that thing!" Belle announced to the screen. She couldn't believe the man was still trying to prove that fathers made superior parents, especially not with this pitiful attempt at carpentry.

"We'll have experts writing the articles, of course," Darryl added. "This is kind of an experiment here."

"So you *are* planning to sue for custody?" pressed the reporter.

One leg of the crib wobbled. Darryl glared at it.

"Mr. Horak?" said the reporter.

"Belle needs to understand that kids need fathers, too," he said as the crib shifted off-center.

Kate regarded his handiwork dubiously. "Are you sure that thing is made right?"

"Actually, the directions were missing from the kit but I thought I could figure it out." Darryl gave the leg a light kick to straighten it.

The response was prompt and startling. A screw flew out, and then the entire crib imploded, boards shifting and falling until the structure lay shattered on the floor. Still holding the railing in midair, Darryl stared at it in shock.

The scene returned to the newsroom, where the two anchors were clutching their sides trying to stop laughing. Belle clicked off the set.

It annoyed her that Darryl had made a point of how fathers were better than mothers at carpentry and sports and camping. After all, *Just Us* was running an article in the May issue on women, sports and the outdoors.

That was when inspiration hit. It didn't come out of the blue; it was more a matter of pieces fitting into a jigsaw puzzle.

The magazine would sponsor a weekend campout for women only! With a little expert guidance, they were going to hike, fish, pitch tents and learn survival skills. It was a perfect opportunity to refute Darryl's point and promote *Just Us* at the same time.

Best of all, it would give Belle something to keep her mind off the fact that she wished he were here so they could laugh about that stupid crib together.

SOON IT WOULD BE Valentine's Day. Sitting at his desk staring blankly at his computer, Darryl wondered whether there was any point in sending Belle flowers.

She would only throw them in the trash. The way things were going in his life, he might as well throw himself in the trash.

He missed her. All he'd wanted to do on TV last week was to make Belle see that the baby needed him, and instead he'd made a fool of himself.

Darryl would never get the smell of sawdust out of his carpet. And he would never get the memory of that collapsing crib out of his mind.

Neither, he felt sure, would Belle.

This ends here, he decided. No more feuding. No more proving himself. He would let time work its magic, and maybe by the time the baby was born in another four months she would forgive him.

Outside his window, the sky had gone dark, although it wasn't quite five o'clock. On nights like this, a man ought to be heading home to a hot meal and some stimulating conversation, preferably with a peppery redhead.

A light tap on the door preceded Elva's entrance. "Sorry to disturb your blue funk," she said. "I came to tell you I figured out who betrayed our theme to *Just Us.*"

Darryl had almost forgotten. "Oh, yeah. Well, who's the quisling?"

"I did a little checking on who might have seen our posters. Then you mentioned that you'd noticed a certain person at Sandra Duval's New Year's party. When I confronted her, she confessed." Elva's voice floated back as she headed for the hall. "I've got the little rat right here."

For one heart-thumping, irrational moment Darryl thought it might be Belle. Then he saw Mindy gritting her teeth as Elva propelled her forward.

"You?" he demanded, trying to work up a head of steam for Elva's benefit. Personally, he no longer cared, especially since he and Sandra were making great progress on their joint project.

"I'm sorry," Mindy said. "Please, Mr. Horak, don't ruin my career."

"Line her up against the wall!" said Elva. "I'll throw the first dart!"

The model turned a yellowish green shade. Darryl felt a wave of sympathy. After all, his magazine hadn't suffered any real harm. "It's okay," he said.

"No, it's not okay." Elva fixed him with a piercing stare.

He didn't want to terrify Mindy, but neither could he afford to offend his art editor. Maybe he could pacify Elva and get some information at the same time. "Have you been at the *Just Us* offices recently?" he asked.

Mindy nodded hesitantly. "Just to take a little Valentine's present to Mrs. Duval. Kind of a thank-you for having me at her party."

"How about giving us a scoop on whatever they're up to these days?" Darryl didn't expect her to know anything of value, but he was hungry for any details about Belle. "You help us out, and we'll call it even."

The model licked her lips nervously. "Um, well—"

"This had better be good," growled Elva.

"There's just this—this campout thing," Mindy said.

"Campout thing?" he prodded.

"Belle said you claimed that men are better at taking kids camping," the model ventured. "So *Just Us* is going to sponsor a Strong Woman Campout in May. To coincide with a special issue on women and sports."

"Belle's going to take a bunch of women camping to prove me wrong?"

"I guess so," Mindy said.

"She can't," Darryl said. "The baby is due in May."

"The campout's in early May and she's not due until late May," explained the model. "That's what she said. She claims even a woman who's eight and a half months' pregnant can handle a campout."

"That's insane," said Elva.

Darryl didn't doubt that, under ordinary circumstances, Belle could pitch tents and light camp fires. But a few weeks before the baby was due?

"Can I leave now?" asked Mindy.

"We'd have learned about the campout pretty soon, anyway," countered Elva.

"She's off the hook." Darryl waved them both away.

The model scurried out the door as fast as her high heels would take her.

"Oh, all right," Elva said as she, too, departed. "I suppose the little traitor has learned her lesson."

Darryl scarcely heard her. His brain was crowded with images of terrible things happening to Belle—a mountain lion attack, a brushfire, a UFO kidnapping.

But maybe he was being overprotective. Or domineering, as she would no doubt claim.

She was a grown woman and had the right to make up her own mind. Besides, he had resolved to make peace, which meant staying out of Belle's way.

Grimly, Darryl pushed aside any thought of interfering and went back to his work.

12

It was the middle of April, and Belle hadn't heard from Darryl in nearly three months. She didn't know what to think.

He hadn't shown up on her doorstep or called to demand that she stay home from the campout. He hadn't sent flowers, or stinkweed, either.

She couldn't figure out what the man was up to. Could one humiliating episode on television have deflated his ego that thoroughly?

In a fit of weakness, she'd bought the March issue of *About Town* and had read Darryl's article carefully, trying to be objective. His devotion to his unborn child came through crystal clear. Belle only wished the man cared even a fraction as much for her.

Her house echoed with the long-vanished sound of his voice. Her bathtub still bore a spilled dab of his shampoo that she never managed to clean. The pans he'd put away in the wrong places somehow remained there.

Thank goodness for the Strong Woman Campout. Roughly a hundred participants had signed on, and a site had been arranged in the nearby San Gabriel Mountains. A female guide had been hired to oversee the weekend and teach the participants basic camping skills.

Belle was so busy that she rarely had time to feel lonely. Only when she happened to see a pregnant woman on her husband's arm did a pang of regret knife through her.

She would survive this. She could survive anything, and she was going to prove it to the entire world.

And so, on a sunny April day, she sat in her office nibbling a red, white and blue cream cheese confection and editing a story called "Personal Fireworks: How to Make the Fourth of July Your Own Independence Day." Sometimes in the magazine business it was hard to remember which month it really was, or even which season.

That fact was brought home to her half an hour later when Sandra Duval flitted in wearing a gray satin bonnet trimmed with menorahs and dreidels. After a brief discussion of plans for the August and September issues, Belle said, "If you don't mind my asking, what's that for?"

The publisher touched the ornaments as if reminding herself what they were. "Oh! This is my Passover hat!"

"Passover?" said Belle. "That's a Hanukkah hat."

Sandra's blue eyes widened in alarm. "No!"

"I'm sure of it," said Belle. "On Passover, there's a special dinner called a seder, and people eat matzo."

"They don't light one candle every night?" asked Sandra. "And spin those little tops?"

"Definitely Hanukkah," said Belle.

A breath of dismay whooshed from her employer. "I have to go home and change. I'm attending a fund-raiser at the Music Center this afternoon, with the mayor and everybody. I simply can't wear this!"

"I suppose not." Belle was about to return to her editing when Sandra tossed back a comment on her way out the door.

"You'll have to fill in for me. I promised to meet Darryl Horak at his office in fifteen minutes to go over the final presentation for Mira Lemos."

The publisher vanished. "I can't!" Belle called after her.

"I wanted your opinion, anyway," Sandra's voice drifted back. "You'll love what we've done!"

Belle lurched from her desk but couldn't catch her, not with an extra thirty pounds throwing her off balance. By the time she reached the doorway, Sandra was out of earshot.

Lisa glanced up from her desk. "Is something wrong?"

"She wants me to meet Darryl Horak at his office." Belle complained. "Then the pink ghost does her famous disappearing act!"

"Do you want me to call him and cancel?" asked the secretary.

Belle was on the point of agreeing, when she remembered that Sandra had an appointment with the mall's executive staff in the morning.

Her next idea was to send Janie, but that wouldn't be fair. Janie, too, considered the *About Town* premises to be hostile territory.

"Thanks, but no, don't cancel," she said, and went to get her purse.

The *About Town* building was only a block away along Wilshire Boulevard. To Belle's irritation, the brief walk left her abdominal muscles aching and her lungs short of breath, due to pressure from the baby.

She wondered, not for the first time, how she would fare trekking along mountain trails. However, the campout was planned for a campsite not more than a mile above a parking lot.

Their professional guide would lead the scheduled activities. Belle could sit around and paint her toenails all weekend if she wanted, except that she could no longer reach her toenails.

Between a video store and a deli, she spotted a narrow door bearing the magazine's name. After taking a moment to catch her breath, she opened it.

Inside, four stories of balconies ringed an interior courtyard. From the scuffed linoleum to the peeling paint the place was decidedly lacking in style.

Darryl owned this building, Belle reminded herself. His equity probably amounted to several hundred thousand dollars. She didn't intend to waste any sympathy on the fact that he couldn't afford to decorate it.

According to a hand-scribbled sign, the editorial offices occupied the third floor. A creaky elevator carried her upward.

Graffiti covered the walls of the lift, mostly humorous references to political figures. Sandra would have had them removed.

It gave Belle a funny feeling, to see the place where Darryl worked. Without realizing it, she'd been picturing offices that resembled those of *Just Us.* Now, she realized how little she knew him.

It shouldn't have bothered her to discover that there were aspects of Darryl's life she wasn't familiar with. But it did.

And why did she feel so apprehensive about seeing him? There was nothing between the two of them. Besides, she was the one who'd thrown *him* out.

He had probably reverted to his old self by now, frolicking in the surf surrounded by gorgeous models. Of course, she didn't suppose he frolicked in the surf in his office.

Belle and her enormous stomach waddled off the elevator at the third floor. No one had redecorated here, either, she noticed as she stepped into an office.

A young man at the front desk gave her a startled glance and hurried to find Darryl. Belle had to smile at the man's astonishment.

She was glad now that she hadn't called ahead. The element of surprise gave her a sense of being in control.

"Looking for someone?" came a voice from behind her.

Belle turned to see Darryl looming in the outer doorway. Darn it, how had he managed to sneak up on her? Now she felt off-center and ruffled.

She didn't remember his being quite so tall. His button-down shirt did nothing to disguise the masculinity of his build, either. He had some nerve, coming to meet her without a jacket. He might as well have emerged stark naked. Now, there was an interesting idea. . . .

A jolt in her midsection shocked Belle into speaking. "Oh! You woke up the baby!"

"I did?" Amusement gleamed on his high-boned face.

"You startled me," she said. "When I jumped, it woke up the baby."

"I didn't notice you jumping," Darryl murmured, strolling forward. "He knows my voice, doesn't he?"

She fought down an impulse to retreat. "*She* knows enough to be scared of ogres."

"And may I ask the nature of your business here?" he inquired, stopping inches from Belle's tumultuous abdomen.

"Sandra asked me to take her place. She had to go home and change hats."

"She had to do what?" He stared at her as if she'd grown two heads.

"Change hats," she repeated.

He grimaced. "That woman is peculiar. One minute she's a genius, and the next minute she's redefining the word *shallow.*"

"It was a Hanukkah hat," said Belle.

"Excuse me?"

"It had little menorahs and dreidels on it. She thought it was for Passover."

Darryl started to laugh. Belle couldn't help it. She started to laugh, too.

"Why would a person even own such a hat?" he asked. "Who makes these monstrosities?"

"Beats me," she said. "All she wore in college were baseball caps and tennis visors."

From the corridor, she glimpsed Greg and Elva strolling by. Elva missed a step as she recognized Belle, but the entertainment editor pulled her onward.

"We'd better get this over with," said Darryl. "Sandra and I are due at the mall tomorrow morning, so if you have any problems with the posters, this is our last chance."

He led her along a back hallway. The place was like a rabbit warren, Belle reflected. Through some offices, she could see doors that opened onto the balcony. Other offices appeared to function like railroad cars, one leading into the next.

"It's kind of a maze," Darryl conceded. "If we make enough money off this promotion, I'm bringing in an architect to redesign it."

Reaching ahead, he opened the door of the conference room. Belle squeezed past, trying not to notice how tantalizing he smelled. Just a whiff brought back memories of sweaty sheets and powerful couplings. Embarrassed to be caught fantasizing, she shifted her focus to her surroundings.

Posters crowded the small L-shaped room. Stacks of magazines held the renderings upright on chairs and tables. No wonder Sandra had agreed to keep the display here. The *Just Us* publisher despised clutter.

The first item to catch Belle's eye was the new motto. "The High Desert Megamall: It's About Us!"

"Who came up with that?" she asked. "I like it."

"Your boss did."

She passed before sketches of manikins in various settings throughout the mall. Ideas and scenes from both presentations had been incorporated.

The overall impression was of couples working and playing together. No longer did Adam bring Eve to Paradise; the two walked hand in hand, sharing Paradise together.

The only picture Belle didn't like was the wedding. "This bothers me."

"Why?" Darryl watched her quietly from one side.

"It's stiff," she said. "In the others, the people seem to have been captured in motion. This reminds me of wax figures on a wedding cake."

Darryl shrugged. "Well, if it bothers Mira, I'm sure he'll say so."

"But it wouldn't be reason enough to turn down the whole presentation," Belle conceded. "The rest of it's great." She stopped as a tightening in her abdomen made her grip the edge of the table.

Darryl hurried to her side. "What's wrong?"

She let out a deep breath. "It's nothing. All pregnant women get these little contractions. It's kind of a preparation for labor."

He pulled out a chair and guided her into it. "I thought you weren't due for another five weeks."

"I'm not," she said. "My book says women get these contractions for weeks, even months, before they deliver."

He swung a chair backward and straddled it, facing her. "Your book? Aren't you taking childbirth classes?"

"I didn't have a coach," Belle confided without thinking, then added, "I mean, I didn't want one. Most women end up having anesthesia, anyway. Besides, I hate pain."

Darryl's mouth opened as if to argue, but all he said was, "I'm not too fond of pain myself."

She knew she shouldn't bait him, but Belle couldn't resist. "Aren't you going to tell me that men endure hour after hour of their wives' labor without so much as wincing?"

"I suppose I overdid things a little," he conceded. "But you should have asked me to be your coach. We could still take a class."

She entertained the prospect for a moment, then rejected it. "I don't have time. Not with the campout coming up."

A lock of hair fell across his forehead as he leaned forward. "You can't go tromping around in a remote area when you're so close to delivering. Just a few minutes ago you could hardly stand."

"It passed, didn't it?" Belle countered. "Besides, I won't be alone. We'll have a professional guide. Janie and Anita are going, and a photographer, and my neighbor Moira, not to mention about a hundred other women."

"But not Sandra?" Darryl cocked an eyebrow.

"She never goes anywhere that doesn't have a Jacuzzi," Belle admitted.

"That woman has more sense than the rest of you. I don't mean to sound patronizing, but what are you ladies going to do if you get attacked by a mountain lion?"

"The same thing a man would do," Belle retorted. "Run like hell."

"What if you go into labor?" he asked.

The doctor had mentioned that two weeks before one's due date was considered full term. He hadn't said anything about delivering three weeks early, so why worry about it?

"I'll be fine." She caught a resigned expression settling onto Darryl's sharp features. "What?"

"I, personally, am not a big fan of sleeping on rocks and eating out of cans," he said. "But for your sake, I'll endure it."

"You will not!" The words emerged louder than she intended.

"I have an obligation to protect you." Darryl folded his rms across his chest. "That incident a minute ago was ot 'nothing,' no matter what your book says."

"This is the Strong Woman Campout," Belle flared. 'Not the Hairy-Chested Male Campout!"

"Be reasonable," Darryl said. "Having a guy around n't exactly a liability. Besides, you can't discriminate gainst men. It's illegal."

He was right. Most men wouldn't *want* to go on a omen-only campout, but she couldn't forcibly eject him.)arryl would probably sue if he didn't get his way.

"All right, you can come," she said. "But believe me, 'll skewer you in my story when your tent collapses."

The reference to his disastrous efforts at crib-building rought a splash of red to Darryl's cheeks. Still, he re-rained from lashing back. "I'm glad you agree. And in e meantime, if there's anything you need—"

"Thanks but no thanks," said Belle, and decamped.

ALANCING A CUP of herbal tea, Belle made a final heckoff of the items cluttering her living room floor.

Backpack—check. Sleeping bag—check. Childbirth ook to study while the others were out hiking—check. he four-person tent was already lashed to the top of anie's station wagon, which should be here any minute.

Stepping outside, Belle glanced uneasily at the sky. A w unseasonable dark clouds appeared to be blowing in om the ocean.

Next door, Moira emerged, toting her backpack. Be-g in her eighties hadn't muted the energy in her step. Ready?" she called.

Belle nodded. "Have you heard a weather report?"

"Oh, they said something last night about a storm off Iexico," reported her neighbor. "But it's not supposed affect us."

Just then, Janie's station wagon turned into the drive
way and halted in front of them. Anita rolled down the
front passenger window. "Did you hear something about
a storm? It was on the radio. We couldn't hear it very well
for the static."

Acid shot up Belle's esophagus, a not-unfamiliar sen
sation these days with the baby putting so much pressure
on her stomach. She coughed and said, "It's not sup
posed to get this far north."

"Unless they changed the forecast." Moira stowed her
gear in the back. "They're always doing that."

As she and Belle climbed in, Janie said, "I thought I
heard something about a flash flood warning in the
mountains and deserts. You heard that, didn't you, Ani
ta? Wasn't it a flash flood warning?"

"Shh!" Anita indicated the radio. "I think they're
giving another report!"

"...and could be moving in as soon as tonight," said
the announcer. "Now here's Joan with the latest traffic
report."

What was moving in as soon as tonight? It couldn't be
a storm, Belle thought. There was no way of canceling the
campout, not with a hundred women due to meet them at
the mountain parking lot. Besides, Southern California
never got heavy rains in May.

"I have this great idea," said Janie as they approached
the freeway. "Let's camp out at Sandra's house! We could
use our compasses wandering through the rooms, and I
think there's a koi pond where we could fish!"

The other three women glared at her.

"Just joking," said Janie, and entered the freeway
heading east.

Conversation turned to this month's Flaunt It Girl,
Connie Sasser. Her stunning photo had been cropped to
deemphasize the other women, but Moira had still made
a conspicuous appearance.

By the time they ascended into the mountains, though, everyone had fallen silent. Around them, the world was growing dark.

"How bad could a storm off Mexico be?" Janie asked after a while. "I mean, that's pretty far away. And the weather's usually good down there, right?"

"They get hurricanes," Anita reminded her.

"With our luck," said Belle, "this will be a him-icane."

The weak joke evoked more laughter than it should have, and by the time they pulled into the parking lot, they all felt better. Until, that is, they took a good survey of the premises.

"We must have the wrong place," said Moira.

"There's nobody here." Belle couldn't help stating the obvious. "You don't suppose the weather scared them off?"

The last broadcast had given a forty percent chance of rain tonight. That was still a sixty percent chance of no rain, she thought hopefully.

"There's a van under those trees over there." Anita pointed.

They cruised alongside. Belle recognized the lettering on the van's side: The Ins And Outs Of The Great Outdoors. It belonged to their guide's company.

As she was about to point this out, a stocky woman in jeans and a jacket bounced toward them from the woods. With her graying hair pulled into a ponytail and her feet encased in hiking boots, she had a sturdy air that reassured Belle.

"You guys from the magazine?" she called. "Hi, I'm Bunny."

"Bunny?" said Janie under her breath. "We're entrusting our lives to somebody named Bunny?"

Belle reached out the window and shook hands with the guide. "Glad to meet you. I'm Belle Martens."

"Bit of rough weather ahead." Bunny squinted at the clouds. "But hey, it keeps the sissies out, right?"

Anita uttered a choking sound.

"I guess everybody else is late." Belle gave the guide a weak smile. "We've got about a hundred signed up."

"Some people get scared off pretty easily," said Bunny.

"Me," volunteered Janie. "I'm one of those scaredy-cats. Anybody else having second thoughts?"

"I've seen a lot of rain in eighty-two years," said Moira. "Never went on a Strong Woman Campout before, though. I'm staying."

"Me, too." Anita's voice sounded quavery but determined.

Maybe she ought to do everyone a favor and call this thing off, Belle thought. But then she'd feel like an idiot if the rain forecast proved to be a false alarm.

Another car pulled into the lot. She was about to wave it over when she recognized it as Darryl's.

There were two people in the front seat. Darryl... and Greg.

She couldn't back down, she realized with a sinking feeling. And neither, she saw from her friend's stiffened spine, would Janie.

13

"IS EVERYBODY HERE?" the ponytailed guide demanded cheerily.

"Apparently so." Darryl couldn't believe Belle intended to go through with this.

"Ready for action!" cried Moira. "Lead on!"

Darryl stole a glance at Belle, who had been studiously ignoring him since his arrival. Didn't she realize how vulnerable she looked, so rotund she could barely walk?

"Wait!" She raised one hand.

Thank goodness. She's going to end this agony.

"Where's our photographer?" she said.

"Don't tell me *she* wimped out," grumbled Anita.

"I'll call." Janie pulled a cellular phone from her backpack. After a search of her pockets, Belle located the number.

Janie dialed, talked into the phone for a minute and hung up in disgust. "She made a wrong turn halfway up the mountain and broke an axle. She's waiting for a tow truck."

"We could go pick her up," Anita offered.

Belle indicated the camera around Darryl's neck. "Why bother? Our friend from *About Town* came equipped."

Darryl's mouth dropped open, and then he closed it again. "All right."

Everyone stared in surprise. Then Greg said, "I can handle the shooting. I used to be a photojournalist before I got into editing."

The offer left Darryl speechless. He couldn't imagine why Greg was willing to help. He didn't even understand why his entertainment editor had come in the first place.

"Thanks," Belle said with a trace of suspicion. "Well, let's get moving."

Shouldering his tent, Darryl followed as their guide led the way onto a trail. With mounting dismay, he watched Belle trundling along ahead of him, clearly out of breath.

She didn't belong up here in the wilderness. She ought to be nestled snug in the couch, drinking hot chocolate as they watched a football game with their legs tangled together.

Ahead, Greg was keeping close to Janie, sweeping the bushes with his gaze as if expecting a bear to pop out at any moment. With a jolt, Darryl realized his friend had come along to defend his woman.

The men were both gripped by the same primal male instincts, he reflected as they filed across a narrow bridge over a stream. They wanted to cherish and protect. So why wouldn't Belle and Janie cooperate?

They stopped twice for Belle to rest. The altitude was bothering Darryl, too, although he refused to show it. He just wished Moira wouldn't keep doing jumping jacks in place and making the rest of them look bad.

"We're almost there!" Bunny sang out every few minutes as they ascended the steepest portion of the trail. Darryl kept a close watch on Belle for any sign of sagging, but she stumped doggedly along.

Ahead, the women topped a small rise and he heard Anita whoop. "Cabins! There are cabins!"

It was the best news Darryl had heard all day. With long strides, he overtook the women. He was right behind Bunny when she marched ahead across a grassy clearing to the closest of two log structures.

In the uncertain light, he thought at first that she was unlatching the door. Then he realized the guide was trying to jimmy a lock.

"No luck," she said without even a trace of dismay. "You check out the other one, Camper Darryl."

"Yes, ma'am," he said.

It was locked, too. The metal appeared rusty, and he supposed that with enough force he could break it off, but these cabins must belong to someone. Most likely someone official with a four-wheel-drive vehicle, a badge and a gun.

"No problem," announced Bunny. "Boys and girls, let's make camp!"

Anita and Janie, who had been taking turns lugging the four-woman tent, dropped it to the ground with a groan in two-part harmony. Darryl unstrapped his double model, while Bunny unfolded her own pup tent.

Belle lowered herself onto a tree stump and made no offer to help. He was glad she had that much sense, at least.

BELLE HAD PASSED beyond doubts and uncertainties. She knew one profound truth: They were here, and she wasn't going to move again for twenty-four hours.

Aliens could land, Noah could sail by in his ark and a Godiva chocolates store could materialize fifty feet away. She wouldn't budge.

Vaguely, she noticed that the men were helping the women erect a half-globe that bore a resemblance to an igloo. She wondered why Greg was being so nice to Janie.

When the tents were ready, Bunny signaled everyone to come inside the igloo to get away from the rising wind. Reluctantly, Belle abandoned her stump.

The seven of them, even with legs tucked up, could barely squeeze inside. Bunny occupied the middle, balanced on her knees so that she loomed above the others.

"Isn't this fun?" said the guide. "What a great challenge! It's too bad it's getting late. I was planning on teaching you campers to fish."

"I know how to fish," said Anita. "You go to the supermarket and pick out what's on special."

"Stuffed crab," sighed Belle.

"Lobster," said Janie.

"Trout rolled in bread crumbs with butter and garlic salt," said Moira.

"This brings us to a little problem," said Bunny. "I was counting on us catching some fish for dinner."

Her words plummeted into a well of silence. Like ancient virgins sacrificed to a cruel god, they fell and fell and left no trace.

A wave of guilt swept over Belle as she regarded her friends. She had never seen such woebegone expressions on a group of faces.

Only Bunny continued in an upbeat mode. "But of course, I brought emergency provisions!"

The mood lifted. "What kind of provisions?" ventured Janie.

Their guide smiled. "Hot dogs and refried beans! Canned corn, too."

"You *did* bring a camp stove, right?" said Darryl. He was being a better sport than Belle had expected.

"I was planning on a big bonfire," admitted Bunny. "But we can eat them cold. We're here to rough it, right campers?"

"I'll eat anything," Belle said. "And plenty of it." Now that her lungs were recovering from the walk, she felt hollow down to her toes.

"Let's eat and turn in," suggested Bunny. "We've got a long day tomorrow."

No one said anything. For that, Belle was grateful.

A LOUD BOOM woke Belle. Rain pounded onto the tent's roof while the thunder faded into a series of low rumbles. That forty percent chance of precipitation had turned into a deluge.

White light flashed through the tent, shocking her upright. Almost immediately, the thunder roared again.

Belle found her heart racing, but around her, the other three women slept on. Moira had put in earplugs. Janie and Anita both lived in noisy neighborhoods, so they must be tuning out the sound.

Her watch indicated it was slightly after midnight. Belle wondered if Darryl was awake. She hated to admit it, but it made her feel safer to realize the two men were nearby.

Reaching behind her pillow as quietly as possible, she retrieved a flashlight from her pack, along with the child-birth book she'd brought. Reading it ought to help put her to sleep.

A discussion of the early signs of labor managed to distract her from the storm. The subject didn't much concern Belle. She felt certain she would be one of those women who drags around for weeks after her due date.

She was getting sleepy when she felt a gush of hot fluid around her legs. The tent was leaking!

She sat up, dismayed. Her nightgown was soaking. Belle held out one hand, but no drops plopped into it, so the leak must not be in the roof.

Patting the floor of the tent, she was surprised to find it dry. Besides, why would rainwater feel hot?

An impossible thought occurred to Belle. She shoved it away. It bounced right back.

Her hands beginning to shake with anxiety, she trained her flashlight on the book again. There it was, one of the early signs: a woman's bag of waters breaking. It could, according to the book, emerge as a trickle or a gush.

According to the book, the breaking of waters wasn't a true emergency. But a woman was advised to consult her doctor immediately.

Well, she couldn't. She would have to wait until morning.

Belle lay back, feeling utterly miserable. After a while, despite her wet gown, she began to doze. She wasn't sure how much time had passed when she came awake again.

Thunder snarled in the heavens, and bucketloads of water poured over the tent. But that wasn't what had awakened her.

It was the viselike grip of her abdominal muscles. Labor had started in earnest.

DARRYL FLOATED UPWARD from a dream, grumpy at discovering that it was dark and someone was shaking his shoulder. "What?" he snarled.

It was Janie, wearing a yellow slicker. "Belle's in labor," she said.

"She's what?" asked Greg, rolling over beside Darryl.

"Having the baby!"

Since he'd slept in his clothes, Darryl simply pulled on a raincoat. Greg did the same.

"We woke Bunny," Janie advised as they crossed to the large tent. "She's gone to make sure the trail's clear to the parking lot."

Around them, the downpour showed no signs of letting up. Lightning jagged through the sky as Darryl slipped into the tent.

The women were awake and dressed. Even Belle had put on her clothes and sat huddled to one side, looking pale and frightened.

"Don't worry," he said. "We'll get you out of here." And he would, he thought. That was why he'd come on this trip, to make sure Belle was safe.

A few minutes later, Bunny threw back the flap and crawled inside. "Bad news," she informed them heartily. "The bridge washed out."

"I'll carry her across the stream," Darryl said.

"I wouldn't advise it," said their guide. "The road down the mountain's probably blocked. Fallen trees, flooded creeks, that kind of thing. Better to stay here."

"I'll call 911 and they'll send a helicopter," said Janie. "Okay, Belle?"

"Okay." She sounded shaky.

Darryl took her hand, and she didn't object. He hoped she felt a little better at the reminder that help could be summoned. After all, the forest service was always rescuing people.

When Janie hung up a moment later, her grim expression sent his spirits plummeting. "They can't fly in this weather. It's too dangerous."

"I can't have my baby here!" Belle wailed. "There's no doctor!"

Darryl's mind raced. If he tried to carry her across the stream and drive down the mountain, they might end up in a ditch or worse. "We need to break into one of those cabins," he said. "She needs a dry place with plenty of room."

A murmur of agreement went up. The prospect of taking action galvanized the group.

Greg and Darryl led the charge. The lock, they discovered, didn't yield to a few quick kicks as they'd hoped. It took a heavy branch and a lot of prying and bashing to snap the thing.

As Darryl shoved open the heavy door, he caught a musty scent and thought he heard something scurrying across the floor. By the time he lit a hurricane lamp, though, there was nothing in sight.

The one-room structure came with a bed, a table, a stove, a sink and a tiny bathroom. At least there was indoor plumbing.

Within minutes, the small troupe had moved their gear inside and piled sleeping bags atop the wooden bed. As she staggered in, Belle cried out and doubled over. Darryl helped her onto the bed.

"I'll call the doctor," he said. "He can give us advice over the phone. Belle, do you have the number?"

"I—I don't know." Panic flashed across her face as she searched her pockets. "I thought I brought it, but it isn't here!"

To calm her fears, he indicated the childbirth book. "It's all right. All the information we need is probably right here."

Two of the angriest cinnamon eyes he'd ever seen fixed on him. "Darryl Horak, for once in your life, you *are* going to ask for directions. Do you understand me?"

He grinned. "Darn right."

He took the phone from Janie and got the obstetrician's number from information. An answering service put him through.

Dr. Cohen sounded sleepy, puzzled and then shocked. "She's where?"

Darryl explained. When the doctor absorbed the fact that there was no way Belle could reach civilization, he began asking questions and giving directions.

The small army of assistants, grateful to have tasks to accomplish, did their best to clean the surroundings. Soon water was heating on the stove, the bed was scrubbed and everyone's hands were washed.

From Darryl's description of the leaking fluid, it didn't appear that the baby was in distress. A thermometer from a first-aid kit revealed that Belle didn't have an elevated temperature, either.

The presence of so many people was distressing her, however, so Greg led an expedition to the next cabin. Soon only Darryl, Bunny and Anita remained.

Anita diverted Belle with accounts of cooking disasters she had suffered. Bunny maintained a confident air as she bustled about preparing warm wrappings for the baby.

But it was Darryl who seemed to reassure Belle the most. It was his hand she squeezed. He was the one she wanted to help her follow the doctor's instructions. The breathing patterns did seem to distract her from the pain.

For several hours, they kept in intermittent contact with Dr. Cohen. They were all hoping the storm would end in time for them to summon a helicopter.

Suddenly the pains intensified and Belle began thrashing wildly. As instructed by the doctor, Darryl reached down and felt something hard and round sticking out.

"The baby's crowning!" said Dr. Cohen. "How's your wife doing?"

Darryl winced at the word *wife* but decided this was no time to quibble over technicalities. "Can't you hear her? She's howling like a banshee. And there's a lot of blood."

"That's normal," said the doctor. "It's time for the baby to come. She needs to bear down."

Suddenly Darryl felt scared. He had never cared about anything so desperately in his life as he did the safety of this woman and this child.

BELLE HAD NEVER even imagined she could feel such agony. Obviously, there had been a mistake. A baby couldn't hurt this much. She must be carrying a two-headed alien equipped with lobster claws.

The more she thought about it, the more likely it seemed that she had been abducted by a UFO and was being subjected to unspeakable experiments. Women would never voluntarily put themselves through this.

The only thing that anchored her was Darryl. Even when she clutched his hand and shrieked in his ear, he kept speaking in low, reassuring tones.

She tried not to think about the fact that he had been equally unfazed while making a botch of their Thanksgiving turkey.

It was Darryl who told her everything was going fine. It was Darryl who supported the baby as it emerged and assured her that there was only one head and no lobster claws.

And it was Darryl who held the little creature while it uttered a wail of protest at this undignified entry into the world.

"He's adorable!" he said. "Kind of messy, but cute."

"It's a she," said Bunny.

"No, it's got..." He hesitated.

"I know a penis when I see one," advised the guide. "That's the umbilical cord."

"So it is," said Darryl.

While he and Bunny delivered the placenta and cut the cord, Belle held her daughter on her stomach, stroking the little girl until she quieted. She felt some pain where the baby had come out, but it didn't matter. The agony of a few minutes ago receded as she gazed lovingly at her daughter's red, wrinkled face and blue eyes.

"She's gorgeous," said Darryl. "She looks just like you."

Belle wanted to protest that she wasn't red and wrinkled and she didn't have blue eyes. But the baby *was* beautiful. So was the baby's father.

At that instant, she felt such a rush of love and tenderness that it could encompass even Darryl Horak. For one aching moment, she wished the three of them would be going home together.

But she knew better than to say anything. The love they both felt was for this baby, not each other. She refused to lie to herself, no matter how much the truth hurt.

———————

14

BY THE TIME the others came into the room, Belle fel'
sleep creeping around the edges of her consciousness. She
fought it, wanting to keep holding the baby.

She also wanted to ask Janie why she and Greg seemed
so chummy. They both looked tired but in good spirits
Only Moira, who declared that she had slept soundly
thanks to her earplugs, appeared rested.

After the oohing and aahing faded, it was Moira who
asked, "What are you going to call this little doll?"

"Susan," said Belle. Having accomplished the monu
mental task of naming the baby, she yielded at last to
blissful, all-encompassing sleep.

THE NEXT MORNING, after the storm cleared, they drove
down the mountain. A pediatrician examined Susan
while Dr. Cohen checked Belle and put in a few stitches
Both were pronounced in excellent health.

She spent most of the next two days in bed. A kind
solicitous person pretending to be Darryl brought the baby
to her to nurse. That same person appeared to have mas
tered the arts of diapering and of fitting tiny limbs into
tiny sleepers.

He had even, she gathered, figured out how to run a
washing machine and dryer. It couldn't be Darryl. It must
be some shapeshifter from another dimension.

On the third day, when she finally heaved herself out o
bed, Belle heard an odd noise emanating from the living

room. She could almost have sworn it was a man singing. Curious, she padded down the hall and peered into the living room.

From this angle, she could see Darryl seated on the couch with baby Susan cradled in one arm. He was offering her a bottle of water and crooning "The Teddy Bears' Picnic."

The baby stared raptly at her father. As Belle watched the two of them, the present faded and she caught a sudden glimpse of the future.

She could see Darryl tossing his little girl in the air and helping her onto the monkey bars at a playground. Then it was Christmas morning, with Daddy in a Santa Claus suit handing out presents under a shimmering tree.

His dark eyes narrowed as he examined his daughter's first date, and insisted on driving them to the movies. Then there was Susan beautiful and serious in a wedding dress, with Daddy giving her away but whispering in her ear that he didn't really mean it and would take her back anytime.

A warm sensation tinged with sadness spread through Belle. How contented those two looked together. Much as it pained her to admit it, Darryl was going to be a good father.

He had bonded with Susan as strongly as any parent had ever bonded with any child. Heck, how many fathers had delivered their own daughters?

With a jolt, she realized that she had come to respect and admire him. The two of them could never get along on an intimate basis, but for as long as they both lived, they would be bound together by the love they shared for this child.

The doorbell rang, breaking her reverie. Darryl tucked the baby into the crook of his arm and went to answer it.

Belle contemplated getting dressed, but decided against it. The bathrobe covered everything that needed to be covered.

As the door opened, Sandra floated in, with Mira Lemos trailing in her wake. "We want to greet the new arrival!" Sandra's gaze lit on Susan and she examined the infant as if it were a bizarre and not-quite-trustworthy new invention. "She's so small! Is this what newborn babies look like?"

The marketing director laughed. She apparently thought Sandra was joking.

"This is Susan," Darryl explained gravely. "She claims to be a baby but I think she's a wise old soul."

"She's adorable." Mira stroked a tiny cheek.

"We come bearing gifts!" From the porch, Sandra fetched an exquisite baby stroller, the kind Belle had contemplated buying but decided she couldn't afford. The publisher dashed out again and returned with a car seat equipped with colorful baubles to entertain the baby.

"You've outdone yourself." Belle moved forward, unable to resist examining these treasures. "Sandra, these are great."

"You deserve the best!" her old friend insisted. "Listen, I know you need your rest, so we'll be brief. I've had the most wonderful idea!"

"It's a very good idea." Mira's eyes hadn't moved from the baby.

"Well, you know, the weak thing about the mall presentation is the wedding scene," Sandra began.

"I did notice that," Belle admitted.

"It's static. It should be the climax of the opening weekend, but it's not the least bit interesting," Sandra said. "What we need is a real wedding. We would provide the most exquisite gown, tailored to your figure. A veil, designer shoes, gowns for the bridesmaids, tuxedo for the men! And such flowers, exquisite flowers! Roses and orchids—I see orchids, don't you, Mira?"

"Lots of orchids." The marketing director brought her face near Susan's and laughed when the baby poked her nose.

"The photography would be first-rate, of course," Sandra continued. "And a reception, catered at the mall's expense, in the Cathedral Court. Wouldn't it be splendid? Do say yes, Belle."

"Are you proposing to me?" she asked.

Her employer laughed in a high soprano, like the good witch Glenda in *The Wizard of Oz*. "No, dear, I'm proposing to you and Darryl."

"You're suggesting we have a ceremony at the mall?" His expression reflected his disbelief. "A real one? The kind you get a license for?"

"A license?" Sandra said. "My dear, no one's asking you to wear a collar!"

"Not a dog license, Sandra, a marriage license," Belle corrected.

Her boss winked. "I knew that."

"If you two don't mind, of course." Mira tore her attention from the baby. "We assumed, I mean, as parents, that you might want to make this legal."

"It is legal," Belle said. "There's no law against being a single mother."

"I think we should consider it," Darryl murmured. "Just imagine, Belle. A storybook wedding, and it wouldn't cost you a penny."

"Me?" she said. "How about you?"

"The bride does usually pay," Sandra interjected.

"Think what a great layout this would make in *Just Us*," he said.

Belle couldn't believe he was going along with this. The whole idea was crazy. But she couldn't afford to dismiss her employer's suggestion out of hand.

"I'll think about it," she said.

"Oh! Well, that's better than I'd expected," Sandra admitted. "Do consider it seriously, Belle. It's a marvelous opportunity."

"Thank you," she said. "The gifts are lovely, Sandra."

After the pair had departed, she turned to Darryl. "You were joking, right?"

"Well, no," he said.

She took the restless baby and settled into a chair. Almost before she had loosened her bra, the little creature clamped on to nurse.

"I wish you knew how earthy and tranquil you look." Darryl sat on the couch, watching her. "So maternal."

Belle didn't want to be told she looked maternal. She wanted to be told she was willowy and breathtaking.

"We can't possibly get married," she said.

"It would be good for the baby." He stretched out his long legs. "She would benefit from having two parents."

Couldn't he say something romantic? Why couldn't he declare that a plump redhead with no makeup and a hair-trigger temper was the kind of woman he'd always dreamed of?

"She will have two parents," Belle grumped. "They just won't live together."

"We could get married for a while." Darryl didn't seem to be kidding, but it was hard to tell. "We could always get a divorce if it doesn't work."

"That's it?" she asked. "How cold-blooded!"

Darn the man, couldn't he see that she would never agree to such a halfhearted arrangement? It would be better to go it alone from the start than to find herself abandoned a year or two down the road.

With a twist of pain and pleasure so sharp it brought tears to her eyes, Belle conceded that she loved the man.

Or loved him sometimes, when he wasn't being so stubborn and cavalier.

But she couldn't marry him, not under these circumstances. It was all or nothing for her.

"I'm just trying to figure out a way to make this work," he said.

"To make what work, the mall opening?" she challenged. "You don't have to go so far as to chain yourself to me, just so they can have their wedding!"

"That isn't what I meant." With an irritable gesture, Darryl stood. "I'm just trying to find a way to persuade you to marry me." Then he got a light in his eyes, a very mischievous, dangerous light. "Wait here!"

"I wasn't planning on going anywhere," Belle observed dryly just before he dashed out the door.

He returned half an hour later, after she had put the baby in her crib. He brought a bouquet of daisies wrapped in cellophane, a bottle of ginger ale, a package of sparkles, a plastic kazoo and a kneepad made for gardeners.

"Are these for the baby?" asked Belle.

"Indirectly." With a flourish, Darryl handed her the bouquet, then set the ginger ale on the coffee table. "I knew you wouldn't drink champagne while you were nursing."

"Good thinking." Sitting on the couch, she fixed him with her most skeptical stare. This was, after all, Susan's nap time and therefore Belle's, as well.

Next, Darryl removed the kazoo from its casing and hummed a fanfare into it. Then he put the plastic pad on the carpet and knelt on it.

"What are you doing?" she asked.

"Protecting my knees."

"No, I mean, the kneeling part."

"I'm proposing," said Darryl. "Belle, will you marry me?"

This had to be his idea of a joke. Maybe he and Sandra
had cooked it up together. "For how long?"

"How long can I get?" he asked.

She thought for a minute. "Until the mall falls down."

"Okay," said Darryl. "Will you marry me until the
mall falls down?"

The man had no shame! Belle was about to announce
that she wouldn't marry him for even one blink of a gnat's
eye, when she experienced a revelation.

The best way to make Darryl miserable would be to
marry him.

He would have to share the hassles of finding day-care,
of coming home to a dirty house, of midnight awaken-
ings and early-morning diaper changes. There would be
no more volleyball games or beach parties.

So what if he didn't expect the marriage to last? At least
he could share the burden as well as the joys of parenthood for a few years.

She owed it to herself to marry the man. It would be
poetic justice.

"Actually," Belle said, "The answer is yes."

The next thing she knew, the air filled with sparkles.

15

THE WOMAN HAD to have some trick up her sleeve, Daryl reflected as he fastened his cummerbund in the back room of the mall's formal menswear shop. It was her air of triumph that worried him, along with the way she'd been avoiding private conversations.

He had tried several times to explain that he had fallen in love with her. Surely Belle, too, had realized during the birth that some things in life took two pairs of hands, two heads and two hearts. But she had always managed to change the subject.

Yanking at his bow tie, Darryl frowned at himself in the mirror. It seemed as if everyone he knew would be here.

His mother, Susan, had flown in from France, and Belle's parents had driven cross-country, her sister having delivered a healthy boy a month early. The staffs of both magazines would be attending, as would Belle's neighbor, Moira, who had decided to augment her Social Security by baby-sitting their daughter full-time.

If Belle wanted to embarrass him, today would give her a golden opportunity to do so.

In a way, he envied the peace of mind enjoyed by his friends, who were donning their tuxedos nearby. Greg presented a striking appearance, aglow from his recent reconciliation with Janie.

Jim kept adjusting the collar as if it irritated the skin under his beard, but he was grinning to himself. Incensed that his ex-wife had refused to let him spend Christmas

with his son, he had gone back to court and enforced th
right to have the boy visit for the summer.

A few minutes later, the three of them took the escala
tor to the ground floor. A couple of people riding up eye
their tuxedos and called, "Congratulations!"

Darryl smiled and thanked them. Despite his concer
about what Belle might be planning, he was in a goo
mood.

The invited guests were seated in the Cathedral Cour
with onlookers leaning against the railing overhead
Flowers and potted plants turned the vast space into
garden.

"Got the ring?" he asked Greg.

"Right here." The best man patted his pocket.

Darryl stopped to greet his mother, who beamed wit
happiness. That was easily explained by the fact that he
new granddaughter, looking like a tiny angel in a whit
lace dress, was lying in her arms.

"I'm glad to see you two hit it off," he said.

"You've done me proud," said his mother. "You g
the order of things backward, but all's well that end
well."

Then, leaving Greg and Jim near the minister, Darry
made his way to a side door that led to a private hallway
He would be walking Belle down the aisle, since her fa
ther had sprained his ankle climbing out of the moto
home that morning and would have to wait near the alta
to give her away.

In the hallway, he found Sandra making last-minu
adjustments to the flower circlet atop Belle's hair. Th
publisher fluttered about excitedly, almost as if this wer
her own wedding.

She had declined to be in the wedding party, howeve
claiming her hat would never fit in. "I think I'll wear m
Hanukkah hat," she had told Darryl with a wink. "Isn

t fortunate I had to go and change it that day? Other-
vise you two might never have gotten back together.''

Crazy like a fox, he'd thought.

Anita and Janie glowed in their rose-colored cocktail
dresses. But today the bride was unquestionably the star.

Darryl felt a burst of tenderness as he regarded his
small, intense wife-to-be. The fitted waist on her white
gown emphasized her newly recovered slenderness, while
a scooped lace inset at the neck revealed a tantalizing hint
of her full breasts. How dynamic she looked with her red
hair and lively expression—and how dangerously self-
satisfied.

In the Cathedral Court, an organ began to play. As
Sandra held the door, Janie proceeded first. From the
glimmer in her eyes, Darryl suspected she was anticipat-
ing her own wedding in the not-too-distant future. Then
it was Anita's turn to stride out with her head held high
and her bouquet gripped tightly in gloved hands.

''You're on!'' Sandra prompted as the music switched
to Mendelssohn's ''Wedding March.'' Belle draped her
hand on Darryl's arm and they stepped into public view.

An approving gasp went up from the onlookers.
Among the seated guests, heads turned to watch.

Darryl felt a rush of happiness. He was proud to have
everyone see him walking down the aisle with Belle, no
matter what her ulterior motive might be. For this moment, she belonged to him.

She pressed close, and he realized she was whispering
to him as they walked. ''You don't have to go through
with this.''

He didn't turn his head. ''I want to,'' he whispered
back.

''I'm only marrying you to get even.'' She smiled at
their audience.

''Get even?''

"Because living with me makes you so miserable," she returned from the corner of her mouth. "You can back out if you want to."

He fought down the impulse to chuckle. So that was Belle's plan! She had said yes to spite him.

"It's okay," he murmured. "I can handle it."

If she wanted to believe that marriage was a form of punishment, he wouldn't spoil her fun. This zany, unpredictable woman didn't have a clue that Darryl was head over heels in love with her.

The hard part would be to keep her from reading it in his face. Thank goodness they were nearly at the altar.

Then her father stepped forward, trying not to wince at the pain in his ankle, and took his Belle's arm. Darryl relinquished her and went to stand before the minister.

"Who gives this woman..."

HER CONSCIENCE WAS clear. She had warned Darryl, even if she had chosen an awkward time for it.

Why was he still going ahead with the wedding? Belle wouldn't blame him if he walked away and left her at the altar. It would serve her right.

As her father released her and she turned to face the minister, she lost her awareness of everyone and everything except Darryl. He stood straight and tall beside her, his strength reassuring.

Relief rushed through her, that he was still here. Maybe he cared for her just a little bit. Or perhaps he figured that marriage would make her even more miserable than him.

"Often, when two people get married, they don't think about the future," the minister began. "When you're young and healthy, everything ahead looks rosy. But matrimony is more than a casual friendship. It's a rock that anchors us, a staff that we can lean on when we need it most..."

Belle had never before wanted someone to lean on. Even now that she had a baby, she could fend for herself most of the time. But the minister's words reminded her that the future was full of uncertainties, like her mountaintop delivery.

Taking care of a baby by herself could be overwhelming. Darryl made it fun. With him around, ordinary meals turned into challenging discussions, and an evening of eating ice cream and watching TV felt like having a party.

Marriage wasn't going to make her unhappy in the least. She just hoped Darryl wouldn't notice that fact for a while.

The minister turned to her. "Do you take this man to love and to cherish, for better or for worse, in sickness and in health, till death do you part?"

With a jolt, she realized that she did. She didn't just want to punish him with diaper duty for a few years. She wanted to keep him.

"Yes." Her breath caught in her throat.

Then she waited for some hint of disdain on Darryl's face as the minister asked whether he took this woman to love and to cherish till death did them part.

"Yes," he said with no hesitation whatsoever.

As he lifted her hand to slip on the ring, his gaze met hers. The contact lasted only an instant. It was an instant Belle would remember for the rest of her life.

In his face she saw all the love that he had been unable to express. Tenderness burned there like an eternal flame.

He loves me.

The discovery flared through her like fireworks, one spark igniting the next. Belle's heart swelled as, for the first time, she glimpsed a future full of joy.

AT THE RECEPTION, there were endless hors d'oeuvres, dozens of cakes, tray after tray of glasses filled with nonalcoholic champagne and an orchestra that played every romantic song ever written.

After a while, Darryl got tired of snacking, quaffing champagne—at the bride and groom's request, there was no punch—and even dancing with Belle. Holding her close under hundreds of watchful eyes and the glare of the Channel 17 minicam only made him yearn for the moment when he would get her alone.

They would be spending a quiet honeymoon in Santa Barbara. Because Belle was nursing, they would take the baby with them. Since the hotel offered a baby-sitting service, however, they could still enjoy elegant dinners and private time together.

He looked forward to walks on the beach and torrid evenings in a rumpled bed. Now that they were married, he thought, things should go more smoothly between them. Small differences no longer seemed important.

At last, Belle agreed that it was time to leave. After changing into a green traveling suit, she leaned over the second floor railing and called to the assembly, "Bridesmaids and lady friends, take the up escalator! I'm throwing the bouquet on my way down!"

With shouts of delight, her friends obeyed. Flashbulbs flared everywhere as the bride sailed downward and her friends escalated up. Into the air flew the bouquet of roses, carnations and baby's breath, lace billowing behind.

Down, down it came, and then Darryl heard a happy cry. A moment later, he spotted Janie brandishing her prize.

"Next one to get married!" yelled Belle.

Beside him, Greg nodded. "She's got that right."

The only thing left to do was to take leave of their friends and families. There were lots of good wishes, and Belle's parents gave them both big hugs.

His own mother waited until the very end to say good-bye, reluctant to surrender her tiny charge. When it came time, Susan handed over her namesake with great care. "Belle, I couldn't be more thrilled to have you as my daughter," she said. "And I want to thank you for naming the baby after me."

Surprise flashed across the bride's face. "The truth is, I didn't know your name was Susan," she confessed. "It was a lucky coincidence!"

"How did you choose the name, then?" Darryl asked.

"Oh, I named her after Susan B. Anthony."

He had nothing against suffragettes, but he could feel his hackles rising. "You should have consulted me."

"Why?" She snuggled the baby close. "You like the name."

Darryl drew her toward the door. "That isn't the point. We're supposed to be a team. Teammates don't make important decisions without asking each other."

Belle gave everyone a farewell wave as she and Darryl reached the exit. "Don't you trust my judgment?"

"It isn't a question of trust," he growled as they went out into the daylight.

Her voice drifted back to the onlookers. "You haven't objected all these weeks."

"Because I thought you were naming her after my mother!"

"How would I have known your mother's name was..."

Heavy glass doors shut out the rest of the words as they climbed into a waiting limousine. But from the way they mouthed phrases at each other as the car pulled away, the discussion was far from over.

And they *fought happily ever after.*

Ring in the New Year with babies, families and romance!

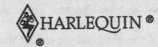

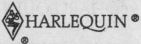

Heartbreak RANCH

Four generations of independent women...
Four heartwarming, romantic stories of the West...
Four incredible authors...

Fern Michaels
Jill Marie Landis
Dorsey Kelley
Chelley Kitzmiller

Saddle up with Heartbreak Ranch, an outstanding
Western collection that will take you on a whirlwind
trip through four generations and the exciting,
romantic adventures of four strong women who
have inherited the ranch from Bella Duprey,
famed Barbary Coast madam.

Available in March,
wherever Harlequin books are sold.

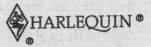

HARLEQUIN ®
®

Harlequin and Silhouette celebrate
Black History Month with seven terrific titles,
featuring the all-new *Fever Rising*
by Maggie Ferguson
(Harlequin Intrigue #408) and
A Family Wedding by Angela Benson
(Silhouette Special Edition #1085)!

Also available are:
Looks Are Deceiving by Maggie Ferguson
Crime of Passion by Maggie Ferguson
Adam and Eva by Sandra Kitt
Unforgivable by Joyce McGill
Blood Sympathy by Reginald Hill

On sale in January at your favorite
Harlequin and Silhouette retail outlet.

HARLEQUIN ®   Silhouette®

Look us up on-line at: http://www.romance.net   BHM297

You're About to Become a *Privileged Woman*

Reap the rewards of fabulous free gifts and benefits with proofs-of-purchase from Harlequin and Silhouette books

Pages & Privileges™

It's our way of thanking you for buying our books at your favorite retail stores.

PROOF OF PURCHASE
LL-PP21

Offer expires March 31, 1997

Pages & Privileges ™

Harlequin and Silhouette—
the most privileged readers in the world!

For more information about Harlequin and Silhouette's PAGES & PRIVILEGES program call the Pages & Privileges Benefits Desk: 1-503-794-2499

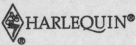

HARLEQUIN®

LL-PP